Here Lies
Nancy Frail

By the same author:
The Deadest Thing You Ever Saw

Jonathan Ross

Here Lies Nancy Frail

Saturday Review Press · New York

Library of Congress Catalog Number: 70–171986

ISBN 0–8415–0139–4

Saturday Review Press
230 Park Avenue
New York, New York 10017

PRINTED IN THE UNITED STATES OF AMERICA

Here Lies
Nancy Frail

1

Nancy Frail had been a whore of a sort.

Whoredom is a business. It has a high level of profitability, the overheads being minimal. Its practice needs only a man with a lust and the money to gratify it. And the right kind of woman. Some of them are craftswomen at their trade: others have all the response and skill of a badly stuffed pillow.

There are independent whores who set a high price on their exclusiveness. There are whores organized by pimps and hired out like saddle-sore hacking ponies.

Whores range from the unbelievably beautiful to the horribly grotesque; from those pandering to the needs of a small exclusive circle of professional or industrial executives to the gutter trollops who consider a pull at a meths bottle on a building site sufficient reward.

Nancy Frail was beautiful and talented and sold herself on the smaller market. She was as far removed from the acned whore a drunken man used tepid and gruesome against the back wall of a pub urinal as the London Hilton is from a shoddy transport café off the Edgeware Road. Both provided a service at different levels of comfort and personal attention.

If she ever rationalized her whoredom she thought of herself as a courtesan. Less slavish than a mistress, more selective than a prostitute, she chose her lovers, requiring total discretion and gallantry in lovemaking.

There were historical precedents for considering herself

superior to a tart but the difference was illusory, founded as it was only on her cultured selectivity and her chosen surroundings.

She had latterly been on intimate terms with Detective Inspector David Alistair Lingard, apparently forswearing the harlotry neither had discussed in other than euphemisms. He, like many another man who had loved a whore, believed he could cage and tame her compulsive concupiscence by marriage. Whether he would have succeeded would now never be known.

For Nancy Frail was dead.

She had been discovered at dawn in a weedy, webstrung lane near the railway tracks. Situated at the edge of town, it was only a few minutes' drive from the flat she occupied with her seven cats.

She lay stiff and livid, slumped in the driver's seat of her own white Mini Cooper. The railway linesman who found her had been too shaken by her horrible deadness to do more than stumble to a telephone kiosk and dial 999 with a trembling finger.

A constable despatched to the scene in his Panda car had opened the door and examined the body without touching it. Recognizing the dead woman, he had possessed sufficient service and *nous* to call Detective Chief Inspector Rogers. Rogers, not normally approachable on non-criminous deaths the dark side of his coffee and marmaladed toast, was Lingard's immediate superior and likely to want to do something about it. And Nancy Frail being found dead in a car was reason enough.

When he arrived, there remained a smoking mist in the air. The bushes, wet and cobwebbed, loomed dimly, their leaves hanging lack-lustre. Busybodying gnats jigged around Rogers' head and he trod wry-faced on liquefying toadstools in the mud. He was very much a cement-footpath man with no particular liking for the country. It

6

was nice that it should be there but he didn't want to involve himself in it.

The car's white enamel was dulled and the shattered windscreen silvered with a fine mist. It had been there some considerable time. Rogers, standing away from it with his fists jammed in the pockets of his raincoat, regarded it sombrely, seeing the vehicle and body as a whole. He noted the freshly damaged wheel arch and the two football-sized holes in the windscreen.

While he observed and evaluated, Detective Sergeant Coltart arrived and joined him. Rogers nodded, not speaking, not removing his steady regard from the car. The sergeant stood slightly behind him and waited. They were following a well rehearsed drill.

To Rogers, the morning was of the *couleur de merde*. Fine strands of web, drifting across his swarthy unshaved face, were an irritation. His dark brown eyes were gritty and tired and pouched from too little sleep. His stomach rumbled its emptiness and he shivered at the early morning chill. He was often unreasonable enough to wonder why the hell people never died during his office hours. Not yet thirty-two, he felt a clapped-out debauchee with none of the pleasures of recollection. He had brooded on his non-ambience with his wife through the night just dead and buried. And had drunk too many undiluted whiskies to help the brooding along. At that moment she occupied a decidedly jaundiced corner of his mind. A small vein pulsed in his temple and the alcohol's hangover hammered rivets in the sutures of his skull. His hat sat square and uncompromising on his forehead. This alone warned Coltart not to walk inadvertently on the shadow of his senior's distemper.

Rogers held a pipe between his teeth, as much a part of himself as his vermiform appendix. Clouds of smoke drifted above the two men.

7

He had never seen Nancy Frail as a living, breathing, warm-blooded woman and had disapproved heavily of Lingard's infatuation, riding his displeasure lightly only because it had been essentially Lingard's business. Officially, she could not be classified as notorious and thus within the ambit of Police Regulations. Nor, in the absence of a conviction, could she be judged of ill-fame and unfitted to be a policeman's wife.

Lingard was a man with a promising future and, had she lived, had she married him, Nancy Frail might well have reached the *éminence bleue* and tortured respectability of a Chief Constable's wife.

Beneath the stiff mask of death she was still beautiful, her amber hair loose over her shoulders. A mole on one cheekbone was clear on the blanched flesh. The unpainted mouth, no longer sweet, was open. A dry tongue showed between lustreless teeth. Her eyes were secret behind closed lids, her face tilted upwards at the quilted PVC of the roof.

The fawn woollen dress she wore was creased. She carried no jewellery other than a watch clipped on one thin wrist. Rogers checked it against his own. It was showing the correct time. There were a few fragments of glass from the windscreen caught in the folds of her dress. He noted others on the floor to one side of her.

He cleared his throat. He thought of what had been until a short while ago the exciting mechanism of shared orgasms and which was now so much cooling muscle and tissue and blood. But he dismissed his contemplation of dead emotions. Their ashes were for others to warm themselves by. There remained only death; a solitary experience, rarely other than obscene. Rogers was easily irritated by people who romanticized it.

'I don't like it,' he said to the big sergeant with him. At that particular moment it was unlikely he would have approved of the Creator Himself.

Coltart waited. What Rogers didn't like would be made clear enough in his own time. To ask was to invite rasping sarcasm and to expose one's ignorance of the obvious.

Rogers' formidable eyebrows were scowling. 'So,' he grumbled, 'we've got trouble. The car's been involved in a collision and she's dead.' He was sardonic. 'A simple matter of finding out what she's doing here and what she died of.' He leaned into the car and poked about beneath the dead woman's legs and in the parcels shelf. 'No tablet container. No weapon.' He slid a flat hand between the body and the back of the seat and withdrew it, examining the unmarked palm and pulling a face. 'No evidence that one was used. No apparent injuries from the accident. Christ! You can't have a crack-up like this without *someone* being hurt.'

'And not in this lane,' Coltart rumbled. 'There isn't room.'

'No, there isn't. Anyway, most of the broken glass seems to be missing.' Rogers spread his fingers and placed them delicately over the top of the smooth hair, rotating the head back and forth. 'The neck doesn't appear to be broken.'

Coltart nodded his head in agreement. He was a meaty man with small green eyes and tealeaf freckles on an oatmeal skin. His fists were terrifyingly large; pale uncured hams covered with a sandy fuzz. A slow and ponderous thinker, his singleminded tenacity made him a better thief-catcher than most of his more brilliant colleagues. The trousers and jacket he wore fell in creases and folds like the skin of an elephant's hindquarters. His suits were loose-fitting, seemingly on the premise that he would grow even bigger and fill them before they became shiny and threadbare. He was a happy man in that his sexual appetites ran sluggishly and not very deep.

9

He peered intently at the upturned face. 'There's a distinct bluishness about her,' he said.

'Yes, there is. It could be asphyxiation of some kind.' Rogers put a finger under the chin and lifted the head up further. The throat was smooth and unmarked. 'Not by ligature. Nor, I'm sure, by manual strangulation.' He shook his head. 'The tongue would be out anyway.' He was speaking around the stem of his reeking pipe. 'Everything about this worries me and I'm struggling. There's nothing logical about it. For a start, she's sitting on the buckle of her safety belt. Assuming a suicide, she would at least do it in comfort. They always do. And why? Have we had a hit and run accident reported?'

Coltart looked dubious and pulled his bottom lip out between finger and thumb. 'I don't know. But it'd be a silly reason for suicide. Unless, perhaps, she killed someone.'

'Check on it, will you.' He scratched his bristles. He was always blue-chinned first thing in the morning. 'Her clothes don't look right . . . too untidy. As if they've been put on in a hurry.'

'All of which could mean nothing,' Coltart pointed out. He was a non-smoker and chewed on things. In this instance, a stalk of grass. One day, Rogers thought, this habit would result in his swallowing the worm of a parasite and his harbouring thereafter a fluke in his liver. 'You're not thinking it's murder?'

'Not particularly. Only trying to fit the picture into the fact of either suicide or accidental death.' He pushed back the cuff of his shirt sleeve and read the time on the stainless steel watch nestling in the black wool of his thick wrist. Its purchase had been a calculated extravagance at a time when he hadn't been able to afford it. That was Rogers. 'Go back to the van,' he said, 'and tell Control to call out Doctor Rees. I want him to examine her *in situ* before he starts his carving. After you've arranged for the coroner to be told, get some screens and the photographer up here. The nosy bastards with nothing better to do will soon be herding.' He tapped a fingernail on the door pillar of the car. 'I want this dried out and dusted for fingerprints. And don't forget to check with Traffic Branch for an accident.'

'Inspector Lingard?' Coltart's face was expressionless.

Rogers didn't hesitate. 'No. It wouldn't help. Later perhaps when we've tidied up.'

With Coltart at the van doing things, Rogers peered again into the car, not touching anything, his fists neutralized in his pockets. Idle hands touched things without knowing and an investigator's fingerprint found at the scene was an embarrassment. To an officer of junior rank it meant also a flea in his ear. Apart from underlining ineptness, thoughtless handling obliterated other marks and dislodged fibres and hairs. Opening the door on the passenger side, he took a closer, more sustained look, his jutting nose with its wide nostrils sniffing up information, his brain tabulating and filing the minutiae of the dead woman in her metal coffin. Layered beneath the fleshy smell of death he believed he could identify the elusiveness of perfumed soap. He noted the slim curved fingers with the unpolished nails, the long legs pressed primly together; the tan leather shoes resting on the rubber matting of the floor of the car. The skirt of the dress was rucked and folded between her buttocks and the seat.

In the ignition switch was a key with a St Christopher medallion fob. He stretched an arm over her lap and turned it. The needle of the fuel gauge flickered to show the tank was a quarter full.

On the parcels shelf was an RAC Continental Guide, a packet with six Gauloise cigarettes in it, a self-charging torch and a black plastic wallet. Opening the wallet, he checked its contents: a three-year driver's licence in the name of Nancy Elizabeth Dominis, the surname being crossed through and FRAIL printed in ballpoint ink above it; a cover note for the car, index number AGL 145B in the name of Frail and expiring the month following, a test certificate issued by a local garage and an RAC membership card. None of which was anything for Rogers to get excited about although the change of name on the driving licence interested him.

The ashtray beneath the fascia was stuffed with Gauloise cigarette stubs and grey ash. Most of the stubs were stained with a tangerine lipstick. There were no matchsticks.

A fleece-lined car coat and her handbag were on the rear seat. Rogers unsnapped the bag and examined its contents without touching them with more than a fingertip. They were a butane gas lighter with a lizard-skin binding, a fragrant handkerchief, a bunch of five keys, a wallet containing banknotes and postage stamps, letters with a local postmark, a tiny phial of *L'Air du Temps* perfume, a tangerine-coloured lipstick in a gilt case and an enamelled compact.

The seat which the dead woman occupied was a clear four inches behind the passenger seat. He checked the adjustment, finding it at full extension. He grasped one of the ankles and unflexed the leg. The shoe on it only just reached the clutch pedal.

Transferring his attention to the outside of the car, he examined the damaged wheel housing. The exposed metal was bright and shiny, not yet oxidized by exposure, although streaked in places with a stone-coloured powder. The glass remaining in the windscreen frame was striated and clouded. A few glass diamonds from it had been trodden into the mud beneath the driver's door. There was a confusion of unidentifiable footprints around the car.

Rogers searched the index of his memory for details of what Lingard had told him of the dead woman before his infatuation chopped short the confidences. Out came the card of total recall.

Nancy Frail. Aged twenty-five years and interviewed by Lingard only four months previously in connection with the movements of one of her lovers, Harry Quint. Rogers remembered her morals being defended by Lingard with more forcefulness than Rogers, at the time, thought warranted by the short acquaintance. She lived alone with seven cats and no dirt of public scandal had ever smeared her reputation. Rogers had been incredulous and non-understanding when Lingard explained that each time she took a new lover she had saved a stray cat from destruction at the local vet's compound. To him, it had seemed a convoluted expression of a guilt complex.

That Lingard proposed marrying her was a fact he had to accept. But Lingard was touchy with his senior about it, obviously regretting confiding in him prior to his infatuation. He had kept the two apart and Rogers was glad he had. No moral snob himself, he yet could not stomach the seeming coldbloodedness of her paid orgasms with the seven men, repeated he assumed at biologically necessary intervals. Her saving of the cats from a saucer of strychnine-dosed milk went some way to soften his inflexibility, but it was not enough to appease Lingard. He sensed Rogers' disapproval and a coolness kept the two colleagues apart outside their hours of duty.

When he had committed the external details of her death to his memory, Rogers removed a slim green notebook from a pocket, unclipped a pen, thumbed it and exposed the ball point and began writing. He filled three pages with his close-packed and large italic scrawl. Occasionally he grimaced at the burning harshness of his pipe. When it made a bubbling noise he held the hot bowl between finger and thumb and flicked the liquid from the mouthpiece. It was a filthy habit, he thought. He couldn't think of a vice that wasn't.

While he was sketching the position of the body on a page of the notebook, a pillar-box red MG bounced over the ruts of the lane towards him. It was an old car and blue smoke came from its tail end as if it were propelled by a badly mixed charge of gunpowder. It was also a very dirty car. Mud and dead flies masked the glass of its head-lamps and fan-shaped segments of clarity showed on the dirty windscreen.

The driver was a woman. A special kind of woman with orange eyes, clear and precise, her straight brown hair swinging carelessly against the creamy flesh of her cheeks. She wore no mascara or eyeliner, only the pale ghost of an apricot lipstick. As she slid gracefully from the car, Rogers turned towards her.

She was dressed in a white military-style raincoat with a tobacco-brown silk neckscarf beneath her chin. She looked well-scrubbed and superlatively healthy. After pulling out a leather case from the rear of the MG, she slammed the door shut, shaking the car. She was Bridget Hunter, Doctor of Medicine and Graduate in Morbid Pathology: unmarried and assistant to Doctor Archibald Rees, MA, MB, B. Chir., FRC Path., DMJ, Senior Consultant Pathologist, whose eminence and distinction she would one day parallel should she remain unmarried.

Rogers raised his eyebrows and then smiled. Perhaps the morning might become of the *couleur de rose* after all.

'Archie still in bed, Bridget?' he asked.

She glanced at the body in the car and then returned her gaze to Rogers. 'He was guest speaker at the Medico-

14

legal Society's old chums re-union last night. He left me on call. I think he'll probably want to die this morning.' She rarely smiled but her eyes creased with sober humour. 'You'll make do with me? I'd just arrived for an early post-mortem when your call came.' She gave him a steady appraisal. 'When I heard you were in trouble I ran all the way.'

'It was sweet of you,' he said. 'I don't know anyone I'd rather have slice me up the middle.'

They knew each other well. Once they had clashed violently, bruisingly, on the issue of sex. Rogers had retreated, trammelled partly by his almost paranoical adherence to Police Discipline Regulations, equating such intercourse with discreditable conduct. He had always regretted it for Bridget burned with a rare fire. He later recognized himself as a pusillanimous fool and in his present discontent with his wife the arrogantly discarded opportunity rankled.

Time having unstarched his stuffed shirt attitude he had rationalised his approach to the regulations defining discreditable conduct, deciding that unadvertised, unboasted adultery need cause no heartburning to an authority that would rather not know that it was happening.

He was not unique in his problems. Few detectives were able to approach the investigation of a crime in a state of euphoric content; not complicated by intrusive worries about either women, their health, their wives, mortgages or income tax. Or all the lot lumped together into a black ball of disgruntlement.

Rogers' alter ego had been kept in check by the dictates of his profession and disarmed by his wife's needs. Now they were mutually bored with the sameness of their responses, needing a domestic and marital explosion to bring them together again. It was nothing that hadn't happened to a million other marriages. He and Joanne

15

were at the beginning of a period of tight-lipped, unforgiving silence over a stupid disagreement. Her brother – in Rogers' opinion the most dreary bore outside the political scene – was occupying the guest room. And had been since the death of his mother with whom he had lived his cossetted bachelor selfishness. Now the house revolved round his overly prolonged grief and his sister was no person to douse its sickly flame or to suggest he should find other lodgings. His indolence and greed over food grated on Rogers' never very thick-skinned sensibilities and he found crime enquiries to occupy the time he would normally have spent at home.

So he was in a mood to ignore regulations and work off his black frustrations in the only way he knew. And that meant with the first bedworthy and willing woman that caught his eye. Anyway, he assured himself, he had had a triple gutful of the same routine of sex. There was never any significant variation he and Joanne could be bothered with and both were conscious of its staleness. So he regarded Bridget with something more than his usual neutered professionalism.

She placed her case on the ground and studied the body, a frown line between her eyebrows. Both were silent. She touched the pad of a forefinger on the flesh under the jawbone, then opened an eyelid. The sightless fixed iris was the colour of a bloomed sloe and the eye, remaining open, gave her features a satirical cast. Bridget closed it gently. When she opened the other she frowned and tapped the eyeball with her fingernail. 'A contact lens, George,' she said. Lifting the other eyelid again, she pursed her lips. 'But this one's missing.'

'Could she wear only one? You know, like a monocle?'

She was doubtful. 'Could be. But I've never heard of it. That's out of my field.'

'Can they be lost easily?'

'Not easily.' She removed a glove and slipped the lens out from beneath the lid. 'It's easy now only because the flesh is relaxed. But I doubt if they'd fall out under normal conditions.'

Looking at the tiny plastic lens on the palm of her hand, he said, 'It isn't going to be a pushover to find, is it?' He waved a hand at the mud around the car, then took the lens from her, sealing it in a glassine envelope.

'You're not happy, George,' she observed. He was standing close behind her. Engrossed in her contemplation of sudden death, his body's nearness was nothing.

'Are you?' he countered. This near, she smelled of formalin and a hyacinth fragrance. It raised the hair on the back of his neck.

Leaning forward, she sniffed near the open lips. 'She's the right colour for asphyxiation, George.' She looked puzzled. 'In the absence of external signs I'd normally plump for a heart failure.'

'In the middle of nowhere and in a damaged car? The facts don't fit, Bridget.' But it was a factor and he worried at it.

She replaced her rubber glove and put a finger in the mouth, sniffing again. 'I thought so. There's a distinct smell of brandy.'

'Take a swab of it, will you. At least it indicates she was out drinking some time before she died.'

After she had wiped the inside of the mouth with a blob of cottonwool on a stick and sealed it in a glass tube, she put her hand inside the dress of the dead woman, feeling the now flaccid breasts, forlorn like punctured bladders. Then she lifted one of the arms a few inches. 'At a wild guess she's been dead six to eight hours. Rigor mortis is well established in the upper trunk.'

'Check on her neck, Bridget,' Rogers suggested. 'She might have broken it in the accident.'

17

She was as deft and tactile in what she did as an osteo-path, her fingertips feeling beneath the stiff flesh of the neck, reading the bone joints and flexor muscles.

'No,' she said at last. 'Nothing like that.' She raised her eyebrows. 'You've no other information than what's here?'

'None. I'm even guessing about the accident she had. But I'm thinking on the same lines as you. That it's asphyxiation of some kind. And having thought that, I've to accept it might be a criminal act. And I do that because I cannot believe she came up here alone.'

'You don't think it might be suicide?'

'What with? There's nothing to indicate she's taken a poison.'

'And she certainly hasn't any of the symptoms,' she conceded. 'But I won't really know until I've examined her thoroughly.'

'You know now why I've a general niggle on me that it's not right.' He looked down at Bridget's adequate breasts pushing out the stuff of her raincoat and suddenly wanted to make love to her. The mere wanting did something to his sombre mood.

She lifted a camera from her case, adjusted the lens turret and took a series of colour photographs of the body. While Rogers watched she spoke her comments on the condition of the body into a small battery-operated tape recorder.

None of these refinements were for the police. Rogers would be required by the courts to produce black and white photographs; despite the undeniable fact that black and white was an anachronism in a multi-hued world. But black and white it had been since photographs were originally admitted as evidence and so it would continue. The photographs would need to be supported by solemn testimony that they had not been fiendishly altered in any way and by handwritten notes made at the time. Rogers had often wondered if it was all right using a ballpoint pen and not a goose quill. He had once, in his youthful inexperience, used a tape recorder when interviewing a suspect. At the trial the defending counsel had, because there was no other defence, accused him of doing things to the tape that would have baffled an engineer with a degree in electronics.

Rogers made a sudden decision. 'I'm going to treat this as murder, Bridget, until it's proved otherwise. Will you check her for wounds or bruising before she's removed? I'll have her out while you're here and when the screens arrive.' He looked irritably at the small knot of curious idlers who were gathering like vultures around a kill and held at the entrance to the lane by the guarding constable.

On Coltart's return with a newly arrived photographer and two searchers, Rogers growled his criticism of their tardiness. It meant nothing. They would never arrive soon enough for his approval. The searchers were trained to find the evidential equivalent of needles in haystacks and to find them expeditiously and without fuss. They carried a stack of hessian-covered screens between them.

Coltart nodded briefly to Bridget. Not offhandedly. Not warmly either. He disapproved of woman doctors, women anything; believing they should stay aproned in kitchens or knitting at home. On the other hand, career women didn't like him either, sensing his Victorian disapproval.

Coltart rarely wasted words. 'No accident reported,' he told Rogers.

'No hit and run?'

'No. Hospitals checked, garages being done now. I've put a couple of our men searching the roads for fresh glass.'

Rogers was neither surprised nor particularly dis-appointed at the lack of information. In his experience, useful evidence came only from the expenditure of time and sweat.

It was after nine now and the pale autumn sun had fired the dying leaves to yellow and dispersed much of the mist. With the screens in position, their metal legs pushed into the earth, one of the searchers laid a sheet of shiny black polythene on the ground. From a varnished wooden box, Coltart took out a bundle of transparent plastic gloves and handed a pair to each of his helpers.

At a nod from Rogers they lifted and manœuvred the stiff-limbed body from the car. It folded in their grasp and sagged like a water-filled rubber dummy as they placed it face upwards on the polythene.

Bridget Hunter stooped over it, fingering the clothing. She lifted the dress above the thighs, examining them, depressing the skin gently, feeling for warmth. She stiffened, twisting her face up to speak to Rogers. 'The briefs, George,' she said, perplexity in her voice.

He hinged his knees and looked. They were white briefs and freshly laundered and appeared no different from those he had seen on other occasions. 'There's something special about them?'

'They're on back to front.'

'That would matter? I mean, it's not so necessary a requirement as it would be for a man.'

She was doubtful. 'I suppose a woman could if she dressed in the dark or if she was in a hurry. Understandable but unusual. Nevertheless, while some briefs do not, these do have a front and back.' She ran a finger down a leg. 'And the stockings. Laddered and twisted.'

'That too could happen if she dressed in a hurry?'

'The laddering? A cheap pair might.' She felt the material of them. 'These aren't. They've been roughly handled.' She pulled off a shoe. 'And the heel of this one hasn't been pulled up properly.'

20

'So I see,' he said, frowning. 'It adds to my unhappiness. There's something so damned wrong about all this and yet I can't put my finger on what it is. It confirms me in not going overboard for suicide. You're really telling me she was dressed after she died. And if she was, her being naked in a car on a cold night – and somehow I can't imagine it – doesn't make sense. And *if* it happened, why should someone go to the trouble of dressing her?' He scowled. 'Or was she dressed somewhere else and brought here?'

Bridget had been examining the surface of the body while he talked. 'No injuries, George, or bruising either. Until I've got her on the table I can't take it further.'

'Will you do the post-mortem straight away? I'm fumbling in the dark until I know the cause of death.' He signalled to Coltart who covered the body with another sheet of polythene.

Bridget stripped her hands of the rubber gloves and replaced them in the bag. 'You'll be joining me at the mortuary?'

'Of course. I'll have her moved when she's been docketed and itemized.' He allowed his eyes to show his interest in her body and she was aware of it.

'I haven't breakfasted so allow me an hour.' She snapped shut the bag, not giving his interest any encouragement. She was serving notice on him that this time he was going to have to work hard at it and make all the running.

She left him with a cheerful wave of her hand, her scarlet car belching out blue smoke, and he turned back to the contemplation of the job before him. The truth was, he admitted to himself, he wanted it to be suicide or an accidental death : an uncomplicated death with its issue as disposable as a paper handkerchief. Murder was an unwelcomed challenge. Each a showpiece demonstration of the investigating officer's competence or lack of it. A successful investigation never demonstrated more than the obvious. An unsolved murder, on the other hand, diminished a man's professional standing. For someone to clear it later, adventitiously or not, was a humiliation not easy to live with. And obtruding into the foreground of Rogers' consciousness was the pressing need to resolve his own personal problems.

While he waited impatiently for the photographer to complete his finicky adjustments and interminable readings of his exposure meter, he absent-mindedly stuffed tobacco into his pipe and used several matches to fire it properly. When he heard the deep rumble of a powerful vehicle entering the lane he recognized trouble like the sighting of an approaching storm cloud and he walked to meet it.

The open Bentley, a gleaming dark green with a polished brass radiator shell, had a long strapped-down bonnet with chromium tubes sprouting from it. Its driver, white and haggard-eyed, his blond hair disordered by the wind of his passage, braked the car to a halt. He alighted slowly as if unwilling to meet the inevitable. He was coat-less and wore a modish dog-tooth check suit with a high-collared shirt and a maroon knitted tie.

Rogers lengthened his stride towards him, waving him to stop. When he reached him he put a restraining hand flat on the man's chest. 'No, David,' he said, his expression wooden. 'It's no good. She's dead.'

Lingard's mouth gaped and he collapsed with suddenly boneless legs on to the rubber mat of the car's running board. 'They . . . they told me at the station,' he jerked out from his bloodless lips. 'They . . . you . . .' He stopped, shook his head as if to clear it and looked up at Rogers. His blue eyes were damp with what Rogers feared to be the prelude to weeping.

'I was going to tell you later.' Rogers felt an irrational guilt and not knowing why he should, was annoyed. He was having difficulty in drawing air through the hard-packed tobacco in his pipe. He opened a smoker's pocket knife, selected a cigar-piercer and stabbed it in the bowl. Then he lit the tobacco and puffed fiercely. The sight of another's grief was always an embarrassment to him. A man's particularly so. He talked quickly, hoping to stave off the brimming over of tears.

'Go home, David,' he said. 'Take some time off. There's nothing here for you.'

Lingard shuddered and wagged his head. 'How was it done?' He wasn't reciprocating Rogers' friendliness.

'I don't know that anything was done. She was found dead in her car. With no indication of how she died. Nothing to show how she got here; whether she drove herself or was driven.' He added carefully, 'It could be suicide, David . . .' He stopped as Lingard glared at him but held his regard until the younger man's eyes fell. '. . . it could be natural causes. So don't jump the gun. Bridget . . .' He halted. Mention of the pathologist would provoke a picture in Lingard's mind of the post-mortem examination with its attendant cutting and disembowelling. He would have seen too many in the past to suffer any illusions that it wouldn't take place.

'I want to know what happened,' Lingard persisted. 'And find out who did it.'

'Apart from her dying I don't know that anything *has* happened.'

Lingard's voice rose. 'Then why are you here?'

'I'm here because nobody can be completely satisfied, David. You know that as well as I . . .'

'I don't know anything.' He stood and faced Rogers, his narrow cheeks bloodless, his eyes wild. He took a small ivory box from a waistcoat pocket and opened it with shaking fingers. He pinched snuff from it and inhaled deeply, brown grains falling on his lapels. His usual elegant aplomb couldn't live with grief. He looked boyish and vulnerable. Rogers' own troubles shrank to nothing beside the enormity of the younger man's sorrow. 'I want to see her,' he insisted. 'To know for myself.'

'It won't do you any good.' Rogers' face was sharp-planed and stern. 'I know you've been hit hard, David,' he said in softer tones, 'but you're not to interfere. That's an order. You can't touch this job. If,' he added carefully, 'there *is* a job. You're emotionally involved for a start.'

Lingard yelled, 'Of course I'm emotionally involved! How did you think I'd be? Laughing my head off! I was going to marry her.' His features were distorted, his expression fierce. In the background the few spectators, their attention attracted by his raised voice, looked at him curiously.

He suddenly pushed past Rogers and strode to the concealing screens. Behind him, Rogers waved a hand at Coltart and the photographer, telling them to move away. He waited several minutes, relighting his pipe and puffing smoke thoughtfully. Then he followed Lingard into the screened area.

He found him crouched by the side of the body. He had uncovered the face and was staring numbly at it, his eyelids red-rimmed. He held one of her hands in his own. With the other he flapped away worrying gnats. Not from his face but from hers.

Rogers waited silently, his expression pitying.

Then Lingard, as if suddenly conscious of his presence, said, 'Her hair.'

'What about it, David? Is it something I should know?'

'She never wore it loose.' He was speaking to himself rather than to Rogers and there was an unutterable sadness in his voice. 'Only in bed.'

24

'How normally?'

Lingard had difficulty in getting the words out from between his stiff lips. 'Piled up, Grecian style. Sometimes in a chignon . . . with a ribbon thing. She never went out like this.' He turned his face towards Rogers, suddenly accusing. 'She was murdered!'

'Look at her again, David,' Rogers said tersely, 'and tell me how. Because I don't know. Nor Bridget either.'

'She's blue.' He smoothed a knuckle on the cold cheek.

'Which could mean anything. Or nothing.'

'But you're treating it as murder.'

Rogers hesitated. 'Only as a precautionary measure. You know that's a standard drill.' He asked gently, 'When did you last see her, David?'

Lingard was surprised, his eyes jerking. 'Yesterday. Yesterday afternoon.' The misery of recollection twisted his mouth.

'You know nothing of her movements last night?'

He shook his head dumbly. Then his mood changed again to anger. 'No. But I'll find out.'

Rogers was sharp. 'No you won't. That's my job.'

'Is it? Is it?' Lingard stood, his blond hair disordered, his tie pulled out from behind the waistcoat. 'Well, I'm making it mine as well! When I get the bastard I'll . . .' He checked the wild words, sucking back the saliva on his lips. 'Never mind,' he ended abruptly. He pushed his tie back into place and shouldered past the grim-visaged Rogers, rocking a canvas screen as he blundered through the narrow opening.

After a while, Rogers heard the Bentley's engine cough on a viciously applied accelerator pedal, then catch and thrash its pistons at full throttle. When he emerged from the screening he saw the tail of the big car bouncing and swivelling in the mud and the departing Lingard being saluted by the constable guarding the lane's entrance.

Where the Bentley had stood were deeply scored tyre marks and the torn halves of a square of laminated plastic. There was no need for Rogers to pick them up to recognize the remains of Lingard's warrant card.

He said, 'Stupid sod,' in a remote voice to nobody in particular. As an afterthought he went to the van and un-hooked the radio handset, calling Control and ordering a guard to be put on the door of the dead woman's flat. He nearly added that Lingard in particular was to be denied access but thought better of it. He couldn't believe the elegant detective could be that kind of a bloody fool.

Then he dictated a message to be passed to the Chief Constable.

Woman, Nancy Elizabeth Frail, found dead in car in unnamed lane off Bourne End at 7.15 a.m. Cause of of death unknown. Pathologist examined at scene. Car appears involved in accident. Coroner informed. Pre-cautionary drill for possible murder. Post-mortem follows. Have authorized press release. Report first available opportunity. Rogers.

He called Coltart over to him and showed him the con-tact lens. 'Put the searchers on looking for the twin of this,' he instructed, 'in the immediate area of the car. Call the laboratory and ask them to run a complete check on the exterior and interior of the car. I want every particle of dust from it, every hair and fibre.'

Before he left, he sat in the driver's seat of the car and operated the foot controls, finding the reach a comfort-able one for his long legs.

2

The constable waiting in the porch of Nancy Frail's flat was an incongruity in the quiet thoroughfare in which knobbed, arthritic trees discarded their yellow leaves gently, almost apologetically, on to deserted footpaths. To Rogers, braking his car outside the tall Edwardian building, it seemed that nobody living in Queen Anne's Road could possibly make much more noise than that needed to call in a cat from its airing. It was all so eminently dignified and withdrawn from contemporary vulgarity.

He joined the constable in the small jungle of potted geraniums almost filling the porch, their dying scent cloying in the October air. Four tiny brass frames containing white cards and flanked by bell pushes were attached to the door stile. One read *Miss N. E. Frail, No. 1* in stylish steelplate script.

The constable saluted and said, 'All correct, sir. Mr Lingard's just left.'

'Left?' Rogers stared blankly at the constable. 'He's been here?'

'Yes, sir. He was here when I arrived a few minutes ago.'

Rogers, badly jolted, swallowed his bile. So Lingard had been that kind of a bloody fool. He cursed himself for his unthinking confidence in his deputy's obedience. Anger against him soured his stomach. He said, 'Did Mr Lingard take anything away with him?'

'No, sir. Not that I saw.' Rogers' anger was difficult to hide and the constable wondered what the hell.

'Not that it matters,' Rogers assured him with the best grace he could muster. 'I just wondered.' But it mattered a lot and he hoped he hadn't made a serious error in not putting a guard on the flat earlier.

Inside he found a white door with the figure 1 painted on it. It was ajar and there was a fresh scar in the wood near the lock to show why. The lock was a flimsy one needing no more, Rogers judged, than a wet loofah to force it. He pushed the door further open with the toe of his shoe. Carpeted steps led to a short passage and into a spacious living-room. The curtains were drawn and he switched on the lights.

It was a sage-green and gold room with hopsack panelled walls and a vast expanse of fitted white carpeting. His first impression was of a superfluity of pulpy airskin-covered settees and chairs and green drum-shaded reading lamps. On shelves, on occasional tables and in niches were figurines and statuettes of cats modelled in glass, ceramics, wood and enamel.

Hearing a soft bumping noise, he opened a door and found himself in a kitchen. In it were seven cats. Real flesh and blood cats, each wearing a blue collar with a silver disc hanging beneath its chin. On the floor were dishes and on a working top three empty cat food tins. There was a smell of meat in the air. That they had been fed went some way to mollifying Rogers' anger with Lingard. He hoped it had been his only purpose in visiting the flat.

He made a hurried survey of the bedroom. Its rank voluptuousness made him swallow. The headboard of the huge unslept-in bed was quilted in white satin and richly encrusted in gilt scrolls. There were heavy rugs making islands of fur on the carpeting. Gold fabrics hung against the white walls. A large mirror dominated one wall and was so angled that it provided an obvious *opéra charnel* for any couple using the bed.

It was a bedroom designed for making love in rather

28

than for sleeping. He wondered if Lingard had used it, savouring his own fornication in the mirror. Then he rejected his own naïveté, knowing there could be no doubt he had.

The bathroom leading from it complemented the bedroom with its feminine luxury. The huge pink bath with its gold-plated mixer tap took up most of the floor space. But it left enough room for more rugs, glass shelves bearing soaps and jars of crystals and another full-length mirror.

Rogers looked in it, seeing himself in an odd, different way; infected had he known it by the sensuality of his surroundings. The flesh of his face was Spanish-swarthy and drawn tight over the cheekbones. His eyes were a warm brown that could darken with anger to a frozen black. The nose, wedge-shaped and thrusting out from the sharp-planed features, possessed an arrogance redeemed only partly by the humorous mouth beneath it. Neither sentimentality nor credulity had moulded its structure. Cynicism had. He was a hard man with little tolerance for another's weaknesses. Burly without being lumpy, he carried himself with the smoothness of a man owning to an unshakable confidence. He dressed soberly and well, rarely wearing any suit but a grey worsted: any shirt but a white one. His ties ranged through a muted spectrum from quiet red to modest green. He needed no colourful plumage to emphasize his basic attraction. It was all there in the man himself. Women liked him, usually for the wrong reasons; first being attracted to his even white teeth and the close-knit black hair growing thick on his neck and behind his ears.

To his credit he never thought much of his own looks, his only acknowledgement of them being his conscious use of the authority and power they carried as a tool of his profession.

He returned to the living-room, feeling the vacuum of quietness, the forlornness that invaded a room on the death of its occupant. Even the cats, he thought, looked orphaned. He promised himself he would do something about them.

A rosewood bureau stood in a recess and he opened it. The interior was a disorder of papers pulled out from the rear compartments of the desk. Someone – he knew it must be Lingard – had searched it and his expression grew flinty, his lips thinner. Sorting through the jumble of documents, he put aside a bank paying-in book, a plastic folder containing bank statements, bank receipts relating to the purchase and lodgement of 8⅜ per cent income unit shares, a desk diary (he noted that the preceding day's space had not been completed) and a bundle of correspondence. He snapped open a leather spectacle case. On its inner lid was a label; *James Hacker, FBOA, FSMC* with a local address and telephone number. It contained a pair of spectacles with bifocal lenses.

A cream and brown telephone handset stood on a table near the bureau. By its side was a mechanical index. Rogers put the tip of his forefinger on the tab marked L and pressed, springing open the gilt metal cover. He read the short list of names on the exposed card and found what he looked for: L(David) followed by his personal and office telephone numbers. He put the index with the other articles for later examination.

A thought striking him, he returned to the kitchen and picked up one of the cats, a fat-faced tabby with unblinking green eyes. The disc under its chin was engraved Rodney with a date. Under the throat of a ginger tom was the name Waldo, also with a date. Not all the cats were so amenable to handling and he suffered a number of scratches in finding them to be named Philip, Jimmy, Andrew and Harry. There was no cat named David. But the name Harry nudged a ready recollection.

He retrieved the mechanical index and dabbed his fingertip at Q. Harry Quint was there, discreetly but definitely recorded as Q (Harry) with his well remembered telephone number. Rogers knew Quint to be a compulsive lecher. He had, on a previous occasion, endeavoured to justify (Rogers never knew how seriously) his sexual activities on the grounds of his having been bitten in the scrotum by an Indonesian warble fly, *Chrysomyia macellaria*; acquiring his ineradicable goatishness as a result.

Rogers was going to enjoy meeting Quint again although he doubted the ex-colonial Resident Councillor would reciprocate the feeling. He thought of Quint's wife, Judith, with her treacle-brown eyes and mellifluous voice that had so nearly charmed him into her bed.

He looked at his watch. Bridget, rubbered and talced, would be waiting his arrival at the mortuary. As he left the flat, so he started to worry about Lingard. Unless he could find him and hammer some sense into him, there was the matter of his contemptuous discarding of his warrant card to report to the Chief Constable. For all his anger, this was a step Rogers wished to avoid taking.

3

'You can't mean it!' Rogers stared at Bridget, his eyebrows down, his face expressing an emotion between relief and incredulity, still unable to believe a murder case had just flown out through the mortuary window.

'I do,' she assured him. 'There's no room for doubt. It's just a plain ol' ornery coronary occlusion.' She was cool and competent in her green gown draped with a red plastic apron, her glossy hair confined in a surgeon's linen cap. She was mopping blood with a small sponge from the inside of the heart she had dissected out on the marble bench before her.

Rogers, doing his caged lion act of pacing to and fro, puffed furiously at his pipe. It was his only defence against the raw stench of the disembowelment and dismemberment of a human body.

'You mean a thrombosis?' he said.

'I mean just that, George. A thrombus blocking the coronary. Have a look at it.'

She put a rubbered finger on the pea-sized black blood clot in the exposed tube of the artery, moving aside and allowing him to peer at it. 'Such a tiny thing to bring someone's life to an end.'

'Not so small as a cancer cell,' he said. As much as looking at the blocked artery, he was regarding her bloodied fingers, thinking incongruously and perversely of their use in the act of love.

'But preferable. She wouldn't have known what hit her.'

'It doesn't make sense. It can't be as simple as that.'

Bridget frowned and tapped the blade of her scalpel on the marble. There was a slight chill in her voice. 'Obviously you aren't satisfied, George. Would you be happier if Archie had a look?' Her orange eyes held his steadily.

He halted his renewed pacing and looked surprised. 'Of course I damned well wouldn't. If you say it's a thrombosis, then it's a thrombosis. I'm just not happy about its cause.' His frustration was obvious. Had he been able to believe it as a simple natural death he would have been happy. 'I mean, she's a young and apparently healthy woman. Not even a fatty. And dying of a coronary thrombosis doesn't explain away her being in a godforsaken lane with a damaged car; her having been dressed after she died.'

32

'She had to die somewhere, George.'

'Did she? Well, tell me what causes a thrombosis.'

'Offhand, the list runs pretty wild. Old age, over-eating and over-drinking, high blood pressure, advanced syphilis.' She was cutting along a large artery in the heart and mentally searching back on the mnemonics of her early medical studies. 'Chronic nephritis, gout, plain worry and bad luck.' She looked pointedly at his pipe. 'Also the excessive use of tobacco.'

'Leave my addiction alone,' he growled. 'It costs me £14,000 a ton.' They laughed together. 'Still, I doubt if any of those apply to her. Is there anything else?'

'You could find out whether she was taking an oral contraceptive. There have,' she said, 'been some disquieting reports of the pill's side effects. The formation of thrombi in the blood, for instance. Some of the pills have a much too high proportion of the hormone oestrogen in them.'

'Would it be traceable in the body?'

'I'm sure it would but it's a laboratory job. We haven't that sort of equipment.'

He nodded at the dead woman. 'Is there anything else that might support it in the meantime?'

'Nothing I've seen. Bloating from fluid retention?' She shook her head. 'Obviously not. Depression and headaches? You'll have to ask her doctor or look in her medicine cabinet. And even assuming she was on the pill, it doesn't have to be the answer.'

'Is there any other drug that might cause clotting?'

'If there is, I don't know of it.' She quirked her lips. 'Shall you and I spend the evening together with a copy of *The British Pharmacopoeia* and find out?'

He smiled. 'Leave the book in your office and I'd be interested.' When she made no reply, he said, 'I think I'll use the Home Office laboratory on this if you'll bottle up the viscera for me. I just can't accept this was an unassisted happening.'

Bridget had cut out a wedge of heart muscle complete with the artery and its fatal clot and was manœuvring it into a glass jar. 'I'm inclined to be with you on this, George. She was physically what my veterinarian brother would call a good doer.' She stoppered the jar and put it in a rack. Then she elbowed a tap on and held her hands beneath the water, cleaning her gloves. 'I can see you're anxious to be done. Do you want the usual swabs?'

'Please,' he said. 'I'd be particularly interested in knowing whether she entertained a lover last night.'

'Call in my office later and I'll let you have a copy of my report. Also some facts about oral contraceptives you might find interesting.'

He was anxious to go. He still had Lingard on his mind. But he found the few seconds necessary to brush the back of Bridget's neck with his lips and feel pleased that she didn't shrug him off.

The Chief Constable's office was a dark panelled room with closed windows and a humming air conditioner dissipating tobacco smoke to form stratus clouds beneath the lofty ceiling. Anigoni's portrait of the Queen occupied a prominent place. Propped in one corner of the room was a cased shotgun and a bag of golf clubs.

James Huggett sat at an oak desk, hemmed in by filing trays, a *Who's Who* and a Kelly's *Handbook to the Titled, Landed and Official Classes*; green leather framed portraits of his wife in hunting gear and his son in a barrister's wig and gown, an unfolded copy of *The Times* and a rack of old pipes with saliva-bleached mouthpieces.

His hair was sandy, wiry and cut too short. The spare flesh of his autocratic face was a newly scrubbed pink. His nose was bulbous and disfigured by a pitted floridness.

34

He powdered it to camouflage its resemblance to a pale strawberry. It was an unearned blemish for he drank nothing stronger than dry sherry. He was known to the more irreverent junior ranks as Old Strawberry Nose, a scurrility undreamed of by him in his lofty isolation. A close-clipped military moustache gave his expression a bonus of a Sandhurst authority. The neat Donegal tweed suit he wore was completely appropriate for blasting at driven game birds.

A black and white spaniel lay on a rug and lifted a lip at Rogers, displaying yellow teeth in a token snarl before going back to sleep.

To Rogers, Huggett was more a politician than a policeman. As he needed to be to survive in his world of trimmed service estimates, a zealous Home Office Inspectorate and forced liaisons with pressure groups of vocal citizenry criticizing the increase in crime on the one hand and denaturing criminals to the level of naughty wayward children susceptible to persuasion and reproof on the other.

He motioned Rogers into an easy chair at the side of the desk. Although smoking his own, he ignored the fully charged pipe Rogers held in his hand. That meant his cordiality was surface and iced at the edges. But neither man much liked the other anyway.

'Ah, Mr Rogers,' he said, picking up a sheet of paper and flapping it. 'Before you start. Lingard has put in his resignation. You know?' He was already making it Rogers' fault, a mishandling of his staff. Man management was his latest obsession; he himself practising an embarrassingly flabby bonhomie with the rank and file, thwarting and blunting as a consequence the authority of his Divisional Commanders.

'I thought he might, sir,' Rogers said. 'You know he had an association with Miss Frail?'

'Vaguely, vaguely,' he admitted. Which meant something more definite.

'Naturally, her death upset him and he's not altogether satisfied that its investigation should exclude him. I considered it should.' Rogers produced the torn halves of the warrant card.' 'He left this at the scene. I don't take it too seriously. He was shocked and emotional. I think he'll change his mind. He was very much taken with her.'

Huggett leaned back in his chair. 'I'll see him, of course, but I want you to speak to him first. He's too good a man to lose this way.' He dug into the bowl of his pipe with a straightened paper clip. 'But now, fill me in on this woman's death.'

4

Returning to his office, hardly aware of those he passed en route, Rogers chewed moodily over his interview with the Chief Constable. It hadn't pleased him. A vinegary Huggett had not been impressed with Rogers' theory that Nancy Frail had died elsewhere than in her car, that she had been dressed after her death or that there was much in it about which to be concerned. Huggett was a glutton for easily assimilable facts and he distrusted unsupported theories. In the process of pontificating on this he had irritated Rogers; never a very difficult thing to do. While conceding the peculiarity of the circumstances in which the body had been left in the car, Huggett stuck mulishly to the unarguable fact that Nancy Frail had died from a coronary thrombosis. Which, he argued, eliminated murder and, as a corollary, any expensive stirring up of unprofitable mud by the mounting of a large-scale investigation. He was so insistent on this that Rogers had, for a wild and joyous moment, wondered whether Huggett was the 'Jimmie' on Nancy Frail's call sheet. He had abandoned the notion regretfully. Huggett would as soon shoot a broody pheasant from its nest as sleep with a woman not his wife. He had, before picking up *The Times* and abruptly terminating the interview, told Rogers he was to ensure that Lingard retracted his resignation. He had been unable to order Rogers not to further his investigations but had underlined his opinion that it should be no more than a routine low-profile enquiry into the unlawful disposition of the corpse of – in his nose-wrinkling opinion – a distastefully loose woman.

On his way out, Rogers had left Huggett's door not quite closed, a thing he knew would irritate the Chief Constable into getting up from his desk and slamming it. The sound of its slamming down the corridor had cheered him a little as he puffed at the tobacco long denied him.

There were two telephone message forms waiting on his desk.

The first was from Bridget and read :

Preliminary chemical test indicates presence of spermatozoa in vagina of NF. Thought you would want to know post haste. BH.

The second, from Coltart, was longer.

Possible stone dust on damaged wheel-housing. Blue woollen fibres area of windscreen damage. Contact lens not found. Glass fragments at scene insufficient to account for holes in windscreen. Witness found, says car not in lane at eleven p.m. Interior of car wiped clean. No fingerprints. Car now under cover pending examination of exterior. E. Coltart, D/Sergt.

He dropped the forms in his 'pending' tray, a glimmer of satisfaction in his expression. Reaching for the telephone, he dialled Lingard's flat number. When there was no reply he left and walked the corridor to Lingard's office.

Lingard was there, his blond hair still disordered, pulling open the drawers of his desk and sorting papers.

Rogers was surprised. 'I thought you'd left us,' he said. 'Are you back on the job?'

Lingard, grim-faced and not looking at Rogers, replied, 'I'm clearing out my things. I shall be gone in a few minutes.'

Rogers closed the door behind him and turned the key. 'The Chief Constable isn't very happy about accepting your resignation, David.'

'That's too bad. I'm going anyway.'

Lingard's office reflected exactly his personality. It contained a well-fleshed easy chair into which Rogers sank. On the walls were hung a series of coloured prints of *The Cries of London*, a steel engraving of The Royal Crescent at Bath and a wash drawing of Beau Brummell. On his desk, paraded in a cut glass tray, was a row of small aluminium tubes of snuff: Attar of Roses, Brown Rappee, High Dry Toast, Macouba and Golden Cardinal. Lingard admired — and emulated as far as the twentieth century would allow him — the customs and mores of the Regency. In his own way he was as dandified as the posturing fop whose picture hung on the wall.

'I think you're being hasty, David,' Rogers said. 'You know Miss Frail died of a coronary thrombosis?'

Lingard froze. 'Who says so?'

'Dr Hunter.'

'It can't be. How could she?'

'That's what I said. But she did.' He paused. 'I saw it myself.'

Lingard abruptly sat in his chair and Rogers knew he was hated for having seen the dead nakedness of Nancy

Frail. The younger man peered at him with suspicion. 'What about her being in the car with her hair down; the car damaged?' His voice rose. '*That* needs as much explaining as the reason for her death.'

Rogers nodded. 'Yes, it does. It's what I intend finding out.'

Lingard groaned and buried his face in his cupped hands. 'I loved her,' he said in muffled tones through his fingers. 'I've got to know what happened.'

Rogers puffed his pipe alight, eyeing Lingard over the flame of the match. 'So you will but first we're going to talk about it. I'm the Investigating Officer and I need information. Will you co-operate?'

Lingard uncovered his face. 'I'm sorry about that.' His eyes were watery but steady. 'I'll help you all I'm able. It can't make any difference now.' He withdrew his tiny ivory box and inhaled snuff, flicking the dropped grains from his tie with a red Paisley handkerchief. Its perfume hung in the air around him.

'If I'm less than tactful in the choice of my questions, David,' Rogers said gently, 'bear with me. It's better I ask you than someone else.'

Lingard grimaced. 'You can't do more to me than has already been done.'

'I can,' Rogers promised gravely. He recognized that Lingard was going to be difficult. 'I know most of the background from what you told me before: the business with the cats; that Quint was one of the seven men. Now I want more detail. Who are the other six?'

'I don't know. I didn't want to know. All I was concerned about was that it had finished.'

'Miss Frail said this?'

Lingard bristled. 'That it was finished? I know it was. Nancy was a finer woman than you could possibly imagine.'

'All right, David. I'm not quarrelling over that. You knew her. I didn't.' *Judas*, he thought, *'what infatuation will do to a man's judgement*. Aloud, he asked, 'She never discussed the men?'

He made an angry gesture. 'Of course she didn't. All that was forgotten, dead and buried.'

'The names on the cats' collars meant nothing to you?'

'Nothing. I never looked at them.'

Rogers considered him a classic example of a man ignoring what he didn't want to see. 'You were seeing Miss Frail regularly?'

'Yes. We were engaged.'

'The last time being yesterday afternoon?'

'Yes.'

'I have to ask you this, David.' Rogers hesitated, groping for the right words. What he was going to ask was brutal but, in the long term, probably cathartic. And, he hoped, a healing surgery. 'Did you have sexual intercourse with her that afternoon?'

Lingard gasped. His blue eyes blazed in his white face, his nails digging into the palms of his hands. 'No,' he ground out at last. 'We did not have sexual intercourse. There was no question . . .' He stopped and glared at Rogers. 'Why do you ask? You've a good reason, I hope.'

'I've a very good reason, David.' His eyes were pitying.

Anger drained from Lingard, leaving him limp and shaken. 'You mean somebody . . . somebody else did?' he said dully.

'I'm sorry, yes.'

There was a long silence in the room. Then Lingard said, 'She was raped.' It was an allegation, not a question.

That hadn't occurred to Rogers. 'It's a possibility, David.'

'It's more than a possibility. It's the only answer.' His

face came alive again. 'That would explain a lot of things.' He pushed more snuff up his nostrils, this time not using the handkerchief and brown powder flecking them.

Having rapidly considered the possibility and dismissed it, Rogers was non-committal. 'But not everything. What time yesterday afternoon did you leave her?'

'At a quarter to six. I went from her flat straight to the office.' He took his notebook from an inside pocket and passed it to Rogers. 'It's all recorded. I was working until ten-thirty.' His lips twisted. 'Then I went back to my rooms. Is that what you wanted to know?'

Rogers didn't answer. He read the entries for the previous evening.

6.00 p.m. Office. Cnfd D/Ps Hagbourne: preparing crime files.

7.30 p.m. Town Centre: enquiries re B & E (Woods, jewellers).

8.50 p.m. Telephone I/Room: check record Charles Wm. FOWLER.

9.00 p.m. Observation on Tico-Tico Club for FOWLER (negative).

10.30 p.m. Booking off duty: D/Pc Vowden.

'No luck with Fowler for the breaking and entering then?'

'No. It's all there.' He clearly wasn't interested in Fowler.

Neither was Rogers. 'Did Miss Frail tell you what she intended doing last evening?'

'No. And I didn't ask her. She knew I was on a split duty and not available.'

Rogers held out his hand, palm upwards. 'Her flat key, please.'

Lingard hesitated, then took it from his trousers pocket

41

and dropped it on the desk. His eyes brooded on it. 'I didn't have to use it,' he said. 'The door had been forced.'

'Why did you go there this morning? You knew that was wrong.'

'To collect some personal property.'

'Such as?'

The blond detective bit his lip. 'Letters I'd written to her. Of no concern to anyone but myself. There's a copyright in letters, implying at least a part ownership. I considered myself within my rights in taking them. In any case, they've since been destroyed.' There was a clear defiance in his words.

'Don't push it, David. I could properly define your action as obstructing my enquiries.' When Lingard remained silent, he said, 'I'll accept they would throw no light on Miss Frail's death. Is that all you took?'

His chin went up and he flushed.

'Of course.'

'Did you examine any of the papers in the bureau?'

'Some. I make no apology for doing so.'

'I don't need one,' Rogers said shortly. 'All I need is your assurance that you aren't going to interfere.'

Lingard's eyes were as expressionless as glass marbles. 'You told me that Nancy died naturally. That leaves nothing in which I can interfere, as you put it.'

Rogers wasn't convinced. Lingard was dismissing both the damaged car and the entering of the flat far too lightly. He had seen them and they must have meant something to him. 'Well don't, David,' he said brusquely. 'If I suspect you are, I'll jump on you. Did you know Miss Frail wore contact lenses?'

'No.' His surprise was a complete answer. 'Does . . . did she?'

'Yes. Do you know the name Dominis?'

'I do.' Bitterness was in his voice. 'That's the name of

her former husband. Park Dominis. She divorced him two years ago.'

'Do you know the circumstances?'

The flap of Lingard's hand made it a question in bad taste. 'The usual, I imagine. Cruelty, adultery. He was a vicious, unscrupulous bastard.'

'Where does he live?'

'I neither know nor care. He's a pilot with some air charter firm.' He stirred restlessly. 'I don't even know where.'

'You mentioned Miss Frail's hair earlier on, David. How was it worn when you last saw her?'

'A Grecian style. At least, *I* call it Grecian. It was done with curl things at the back.' He made circles with his forefinger; vaguely, helplessly. 'Worn high at the back of her head.'

'How was she dressed?'

'As she was this morning.' The dark shadow of sad recollection crossed his face.

'Did she use the safety belt in her car?'

'Always. She had a thing about the possibility of scarring her face in an accident.'

Rogers searched his memory for other matters and, finding none, asked, 'Is there nothing else you can tell me, David?'

He stared at Rogers sombrely. 'No. You've asked me all these questions. Now tell me why, if Nancy's death is the natural one you say it is.'

Rogers looked in the bowl of his pipe as if seeking guidance. He chose his words carefully. 'I'm satisfied about the cause of her death. I'm not with the circumstances surrounding it. Somebody drove her to the lane and left her there. The car, as you noticed, had been involved in a collision. That, so far, remains unexplained.' He gestured irritably. 'You know most of this yourself.'

He waited for Lingard's reply. When he said nothing, Rogers continued. 'About the matter of your resignation, David. Will you now reconsider it? It doesn't help either the enquiry or your future for you to go charging off in a dudgeon.' His voice softened. 'I know the worst possible thing is inaction in something with which you are personally concerned but you've got to leave it with me to sort out.'

Lingard's head was bowed, his chin flattening his tie, his eyelids shuttering whatever was in his mind from Rogers' observation. Then his head jerked up, his eyes open and cold. 'Bollocks to my future and stuff the bloody service. Bollocks to you too, Rogers. You've never bothered to hide your jealousy. So far as you were concerned...'

'Jealousy?' Rogers' face darkened as he interrupted Lingard. 'Are you mad? Jealous over th...' He swallowed the contempt he was about to unleash, breathing heavily through his nostrils. 'I'm telling you now,' he warned him harshly. 'Don't interfere.'

Lingard stood. Despair had made him a dangerous and unpredictable animal. 'My resignation stays where it is. On Huggett's desk. So don't tell me what I can or can't do.'

Rogers pushed himself out of his chair. He was pale with anger and near explosion point. 'All right, David. Man to man if that's the way you want it. The woman was a bloody whore and you know it. I believe she was knocking it off while you were supposed to be engaged to her. You're a fool if you think differently.' His knuckles were balled, ready for him.

Lingard was shaking but he rounded the desk in a sudden rush.

Rogers knocked aside the wildly swung fist and hit him a paralysing blow on the bottom button of his silk-figured waistcoat, stopping him dead. Lingard's face was contorted agony, his mouth opening with the outrush of his breath.

Grabbing a handful of collar and tie, Rogers pushed him hard into the chair he had himself just vacated. He waited while the other man struggled to breathe. When the blue eyes opened in his cheese-coloured face and he groaned, Rogers said, 'That was just between you and me, David. Pack your things and get out. I'll tell the Chief Constable you're taking the leave you're entitled to and won't be back.'

When he closed the door behind him he realized he was trembling, his anger not yet gone from him. He returned to his own office and retrieved the two message forms from the 'pending' tray, locking them in one of the desk drawers. From another drawer he took a bottle and poured out a whisky. He drank this undiluted before going to see Huggett.

He didn't fool himself that the Chief Constable was going to be very pleased to hear the news about his blue-eyed boy.

Before calling on Bridget at the hospital, Rogers mowed his whiskers with a spare shaver operated from his car battery, not slowing the car appreciably to do it.

Bridget was typing her report when he arrived. She rolled it from the machine, signed a carbon copy and handed it to him.

'I'm glad you shaved,' she said. 'You were beginning to look like the late Che Guevara.'

'And feeling like him. Do you happen to have a bottle of skin conditioner in your filing cabinet?'

'It's sherry,' she said. 'I'll pour you one while you read my report.'

He perched on the corner of her desk and read it. Addressed to Her Majesty's Coroner, it was headed

45

PRELIMINARY REPORT.

Name of Deceased: Nancy Elizabeth FRAIL.
Apparent Age: 25 years.   Height: 5′ 4″ (160cm 25mm).
Hair: Fair; long and straight. Pubic hair matching head hair.
Teeth: Dental chart attached.

'You've worked fast, Bridget,' he observed, taking the glass of sherry from her. He lifted it in salute. '*Gesundheit!* as we Deutschlanders have it.'

'Only for you, George.' She was wearing a blue linen dress, taut across her flat belly and outlining her thighs. To Rogers she looked eminently edible.

He read on.

EXTERNAL EXAMINATION. *The body of a young, lightly built adult female. It was clothed in a fawn woollen dress with a belt, a silk slip, white briefs, a suspender belt, stockings and tan shoes. The briefs were worn back to front: the stockings twisted, one not being fully on. The clothing was all better-than-average quality. A watch was worn on the left wrist and was showing the correct time. There were no finger rings or costume jewellery. The fingernails were long and unpolished, their condition suggesting a sedentary occupation.*

The body was lying in the driving seat of a Mini Cooper car. The arms were relaxed, the hands resting on the thighs. Both knees were flexed, the feet on the floor. The head was tilted back at an approximate angle of 45°. Rigor mortis was present in all limbs.

There was a blue discolouration of the lips and both ears. The eyes were closed. The right eye was fitted with a contact lens. None was evident in the left.

46

INTERNAL EXAMINATION.

Thorax: The trachea, bronchi, lungs and pleura were normal.

The Heart: All chambers were dilated. The muscles and valves appeared healthy. There was no evidence of atheromatous degeneration in the coronary arteries but the lumen of the left coronary was blocked one inch from its origin by a clot.

Abdomen: The liver, spleen, pancreas, kidneys, suprarenals and intestines were normal. The stomach contained about six ounces of well-digested food. There was no smell of alcohol. A vaginal swab subjected to Barberio's test (picric acid) produced typical yellow-tinted rhomboid needles indicative of the presence of male sperm.

Skull and contents: No damage was present to the cranium and there was no evidence of any intercranial abnormality. The vertebrae were intact, showing no damage.

Opinion: Death in my opinion was due to coronary thrombosis, the post-mortem appearances being compatible with death occurring between 10 p.m. and midnight prior to my examination.

(sgd) Bridget Jane Hunter, MD, MRC (Path).

Rogers folded the report and put it in his pocket. 'Were the spermatazoa alive and kicking, Bridget? Or does the picric acid stun them?'

She smiled. 'You'll have to wait for me to do a stained preparation to identify them at all. I believe them to be fresh only because I found the majority in the vestibule of the vagina.'

'Foreign territory to me, Bridget,' he said solemnly. 'I assume it means there was very little time for dispersion?'

'Yes, but don't let me mislead you. Although I'm fairly

47

certain, I can be wrong. What I found could be tricho-
monads which aren't uncommon phenomena in a woman
and mean nothing at all.' She was putting the sherry bottle
back in the filing cabinet drawer. 'I did a Barberio's test
only because it can be done in a few minutes.'

'I love you for it,' he said, sliding off the desk and standing behind her. When he saw she was waiting for him, he
put his arms under her armpits and cupped her breasts.
She twisted in his arms and faced him, her body pliant
and responding, burning against his through the thin
linen dress. His voice was unsteady. 'Under these flimsy
bits of haberdashery you aren't so cool and clinical, are
you?' He nuzzled aside her hair and kissed the warm
throat. Beneath the perfume she wore he could detect the
ghost of a ghost of a whiff of formalin.

She put her hands flat against the lapels of his jacket,
her body arched into his, looking at him gravely. 'Is it the
sherry, George? Or do I actually have a definite bio-
logical effect on you?'

'You do. Highly aphrodisiacal. My pulse keeps slipping
a cog.'

'I was beginning to think you a neuter. After the last
time . . .' Dark orange lights were in her eyes. The last
time had been an embarrassing fiasco for both of them.

'Normally I'm as frigid as an Eskimo's back porch,' he
lied. He touched her mouth gently with his own. Then he
looked at the uncurtained windows and the unlocked
door. 'Should we not fear discovery *flagrante delicto*? And
with the sun still shining.' He unhitched himself from her
and moved away. He was physically moved and showed it.
'Judas, Bridget. Keep at least a yard from me at your peril.'

'Would you be interested in another sherry, George?'

He pulled back his shirt sleeve and looked at his watch.
'Not now, Bridget. I'm due at the Frail flat. The laboratory
people are doing a check on it for me.'

48

'I didn't mean now,' she said calmly. 'I meant later.'

He had a suffocating feeling in his chest but his face was impassive. He had reached his watershed and he splashed through it. 'You mean later like about ten o'clock? When I'm possibly finished?'

'Yes.' She held his regard without coquetry. 'You know the way up.'

As he opened the door to leave, she held out a folded pad of papers. 'You forgot these, George. Everything you'll ever need to know about oral contraceptives.'

5

Rogers' desk, normally of a regimented neatness, was now a disorder of papers and items taken from Nancy Frail's flat and from her car. Here were the significant statistics and artifacts of her life for Rogers to pore over and interpret as best he could. Among them were other artifacts; those of his hurried lunch: an empty coffee container, sandwich wrappings and coiled orange peel.

Of the more interesting items found in the bathroom medicine cabinet had been a small cardboard box. Rogers read its inscription: *PROESTOLIN* ♀ *: fifteen tablets. Progestogen 2 mgms. Oestrogen 100 microgrms. Mestranol. Norethynodrel.* It supported Bridget's hypothesis that the probable cause of Nancy Frail's thrombus was her use of an oral contraceptive.

Rogers smoked his pipe continuously, refuelling and lighting it without conscious thought as he checked through the exhibits.

A newspaper clipping dated eighteen months previously and pinned to a handwritten letter caught his attention. The clipping referred to a Sir Andrew Wallace JP of Spye

Green Hall opening a philatelic exhibition in aid of The Commonwealth Cancer Research Fund and, among a plethora of platitudes, expressing a lifelong interest in nineteenth-century postage stamps with a self-confessed obsession with the French *Classiques*.

The letter, dated six days after the clipping, read:

Dear Miss Frail,

Thank you. I would, indeed, appreciate viewing your collection. From the description you give they undoubtedly include the 1852 and 1853–1860 issues of President Louis Napoleon and these would, of course, be of particular interest to me. Would you prefer I call at your address?

Yours sincerely,
Andrew Wallace

The mechanical telephone index yielded seven entries (excluding Lingard's) identified – and thereby made significant – only by an initial and a bracketed first name. He jotted them on his scratch pad as he found them:

G(Donald): 31881. G(Philip): 22430. H(Jimmy): 21206. J(Rodney): 24319. N(Waldo): 33764. Q(Harry): 21618. W(Andrew): 23222.

He opened the spectacle case and rechecked the inscription inside: *James Hacker, FBOA, FSMC* with the telephone number given as 21206. Although he felt a tiny spark of regret for the final elimination of the Chief Constable as 'Jimmy', he was pleased at identifying Hacker. He knew him slightly although only by repute. He had been described as a hard-living, hard-drinking handsome bachelor, very popular with women between fifteen and fifty with occasional forays into age groups outside that limit. Rogers had never considered him as needing to pay for their favours.

It required no mental gymnastics to equate the

philatelic-minded Sir Andrew Wallace with the entry W(Andrew).

Without lifting the receiver of his internal telephone, he twice depressed the red switch labelled Coltart. When the huge sergeant entered the office, chewing the end of a wooden pencil, Rogers wrote the telephone numbers on a piece of paper and gave it to him. 'Go and see the Head Postmaster, sergeant, and screw the names of the subscribers owning these numbers out of him. He'll tell you it's against the rules and Holy Writ but that's only a vestigial twitch from his union days. He's very co-operative if you ignore his first two refusals. But before you see him, lay on two of the plain clothes aids to do a house-to-house enquiry in Queen Anne's Road. Don't advertise it. The Chief Constable thinks we're wasting our time.' He rubbed the ball of his thumb against the grain of his newly emerging chin stubble. 'Probably we are but I'm in the mood to be bloody-minded.'

Coltart spat a splinter of pencil on to Rogers' carpet. 'For what it's worth,' he said diffidently, 'I've a theory.'

'Thank God for that,' Rogers said without sarcasm. 'I'm glad some bugger has. *I* haven't.'

Coltart blinked. 'She's driving her car with her married boy-friend on board. They've done their thing and she's taking him home. Then she has her heart attack and piles the car into a wall. Chummy in the passenger seat puts his head through the windscreen but does no damage, except perhaps to his bowler hat. Which wouldn't be unusual, the glass being made that way. So now chummy's in a real fix. He can't leave her dead in the middle of the road. She'd be found straight away. So he panics, gets her out of her safety belt and into the passenger seat, knocks a hole in his side of the glass for visibility and drives to the nearest lane to his own place. Then he replaces her in the driving seat, forgetting to do up the safety belt, and walks home.'

·What about the windscreen glass all over the road,'
Rogers pointed out. 'So far you've been unable to find it.'

'He could have spent a minute or two brushing it into a
ditch. We'd never find it there. Or the wall could have
been on a verge. We haven't checked the grass edges.'

There was a long silence in the office while Rogers
brooded on it. Then he said, 'I warned you I was bloody-
minded, sergeant. I'll take the likely arguments against its
feasibility, not because I necessarily disagree with you but
to give it a good airing. First, her clothing. According to
Doctor Hunter – and she's the expert on how to wear
them, not you or I – the briefs were on back to front. Also
the stockings were disarranged.'

'She'd had sexual intercourse,' Coltart said, his oatmeal
eyebrows heavily disapproving, 'and I'm told the removal
of briefs facilitates it. Their being wrongly put back on
doesn't seem unusual to me. The same goes for the
stockings. They would have to be unhitched from the
girdle thing she wore.'

Rogers eyed his sergeant with ironic amusement.
'Casanova Coltart,' he derided him. 'I suppose I'll have to
defer to your detailed experience in such matters. All
right, what about the missing contact lens? No, don't
bother.' He stopped him answering. 'That's too simple.
There can't be any significance in its loss, only in where
it might be found.'

'It's such a small thing; so difficult to actually see,'
Coltart said, 'that its not being found means nothing.'

'Her hair,' Rogers continued. 'I'm reliably informed she
wore it loose only in bed.'

The sergeant's deep green eyes glittered. 'I understand
sexual intercourse in a small car can involve a fair bit of
thrashing about.' He was unsmiling, stating what was to
him a disgusting fact. 'Would it be so unusual for her hair
to have become undone?'

'I suppose not. But wouldn't there have been pins or one of those tortoiseshell comb things in the car?'

'There weren't, I'll admit. But the intercourse could have taken place behind a hedge, in a hay rick . . . anywhere.'

Rogers snorted. 'Not with a woman like Nancy Frail, sergeant. You're thinking of a thirty-bob transport café job. Knee-tremblers. I know your idea of a whore. She's someone with a tight skirt up around her buttocks, fishnet stockings and a shiny black handbag as big as a suitcase. She'd wear an ankle chain, two-inch nylon eyelashes and her face enamelled like a repainted secondhand jalopy.'

Coltart's expression remained unchanged. 'I've seen one or two. They've also snakes tattooed on their arms.'

'The universal phallic motif,' Rogers said. 'Well, there are others. My own assessment of Frail is a woman demanding silk sheets, a pre-performance shower in Chanel No. 5 and a fair amount of ritualistic gallantry to deodorize what she was doing.' He shook his head. 'If she ever did it in the back seat of a Mini Cooper or in a haystack, then I've learned nothing about women in all my thirty-one years.'

Coltart possessed a suety streak of stubbornness. 'I read last week of a well-known actress being caught knocking it off in a back row seat of a Hollywood cinema with her ex-husband's chauffeur. So it does happen.'

'I know of the lady,' Rogers said carelessly. 'She was a Grade A nymphomaniac when Errol Flynn was around to do something about it. If it hadn't been the chauffeur it would have been the cinema commissionaire. And she'd even pay if she couldn't get it any other way. She's just a woman who likes sweaty undershirts. But,' he hastened to say with a placatory smile, 'there's a lot of merit in what you say and you could be so right. It's just I'm not in the mood to agree with anybody at the moment.' He looked puzzled. 'But why bring in the bowler hat?'

Coltart screwed his small eyes up in a spasm of humour. 'I put that in to give my theory some sort of respectability.'

Neither man had mentioned Lingard but he was very much in their minds.

With Coltart on his way to the Head Postmaster, Rogers dialled the number of the Blakehill Airport Police Authority. He spoke to Godson, the duty Chief Inspector, asking him to do an unpublicized check on the pilots' records for the details and background of Park Dominis.

'I know him, George,' Godson said, 'but having company with me I'll call back.'

The bank paying-in slips Rogers thumbed through were interesting. Checking back two years, he found that Quint had, until four months previously, paid twenty-two sums of £5 by cheque; 'DG', fifteen of £10; Hacker, twelve of £10 and 'AW' one of £850 eighteen months previously. Quint, Rogers thought, appeared to be getting it with a discount; being the only one paying amounts of £5.

There were no cheque payments in respect of 'RJ', 'PG' or 'WN' and Rogers assumed they had merely shown more discretion than the others, paying their way in unidentifiable bank notes. There were bankings of a number of sums of £10 and its multiples to support this.

The bank statements, addressed to Nancy Elizabeth Frail, 1(a) Bushey House, Queen Anne's Road, revealed she was receiving monthly payments of £100 from P. Dominis and a small regular income from unit shares in concerns indicated cryptically as INT. BRI. FD and AUST. C.N. CORP.

Rogers did a rapid casting of the figures and assessed her annual income to be only a little short of £2500 which, he thought, a not inconsiderable amount to be garnered from an end biblically condemned as being

54

bitter as wormwood and sharp as a two-edged sword. Furthermore, on this occasion it had proved as lethal.

The desk diary contained little that was comprehensible at first reading. The same sets of initials occurred at regular intervals, most coinciding closely with the payments of cheques or cash into her account. After each pair of initials appeared the notations (a) or (h). Quint's initials did not appear after June. Nor the initials 'RJ' after April. One entry for 'AW', a month previously, had the words *Rajput Cat* bracketed after it. There were a number of entries recording 'DL', all within the past four months. Some, Rogers noted cynically and without surprise, on the same dates she had entertained one or other of her paying guests. They justified his harsh words to Lingard and to that extent buttered his gritty conscience.

He tabulated his findings, hoping they would mean something:

Recordings since Jan 1	Number of visits	Cheques paid over period of two years	Notes
RJ (h)	6	None	No diary entries after 6th April
PG (h)	9	None	Last visit 1st October
JH (a) and (h)	7	£120	Identified James HACKER. Last visit 5th October
AW (a) and (h)	8	£850	Single cheque. Last visit 16th September
HQ (a) and (h)	12	£110	Identified Harry QUINT. No diary entries after 2nd June
DG (h)	5	£150	Last visit 4th September
WN (h)	9	None	Last visit 11th October, day before NF's death

Judas, Rogers marvelled under his breath, *but she must have been accomplished. Certainly hard-working. And no income tax to pay on it either.*

Most of the remaining entries referred to twice-weekly appointments with a Monsieur Paul (whom Rogers quickly disposed of as her hairdresser) and three-monthly checks with her dentist who, fortunately for him, possessed initials entirely dissimilar from any recorded. There were reminders for renewals of licences and subscriptions and theatre and orchestral engagements.

There were no diaries for the previous years nor, in her desk, had there been any correspondence other than gossipy reams of paralysing dullness and rectitude from other women.

In her wallet was a £10 note, several £1 notes, correspondence and bills. The letters – from a woman friend Cynthia – were chatty and uninformative.

Like a black cloud boiling up over an otherwise clear horizon, Rogers' case-hardened cynicism was insisting that the worst was yet to come.

His friend, Godson, from Blakehill went some way in justifying his gloomy view. 'This chap Dominis,' he told Rogers over the telephone, 'is a Flight Captain with the Concordant-Global Airways, flying DC8s. I remember him because a few weeks ago he took a boozy swing at his navigation officer in the crews' bar here at the airport. He nearly tore his head off. A nasty-tempered cove, so I understand. But popular with the ladies. And proficient enough at flying to get away with anything short of murder.'

'That sounds good, Bill. What's his form?'

'An ex-Squadron Leader with an AFC after his name. He refused to bale out of an experimental tactical fighter that was dropping him and a couple of million pounds worth of secret ironmongery into the Irish Sea. He landed

56

it more or less intact on a strip of beach just long enough for a No. 2 iron shot. By all accounts he's got guts enough for two. Let me see . . .'

Rogers heard him turning over paper at the other end. 'Ah, yes. He's thirty-two and married to one Mrs Nancy Elizabeth Dominis with the unlikely maiden name of Frail. *Frailty, thy name is woman,*' he quoted and laughed.

Rogers laughed with him. It was a time for being polite. 'Go on, Bill,' he said. 'This is very interesting.'

'No children and they live at 18 Broken Cross, High Moor. He runs a black Sunbeam Stiletto, index number Q361KAM. His personal description: six feet two inches, heavy build, black hair and moustache, brown eyes, prominent scar on left temple – that's the one he collected earning his AFC.' Godson neutralized his voice. 'Is he in trouble, George? Something I should know about?'

'I don't honestly know, Bill. I'm in the process of digging out backgrounds on a sudden death enquiry. When you're passing the office, drop in and I'll explain. In the meantime, don't fret. There's nothing you need report to your headquarters yet.'

When he put the telephone down he said aloud, 'Married! The bitch was still married!' It was Lingard he was most concerned about. The scars were going to last a long time.

When Coltart entered the office, it was with a broad grin on his freckled face. The shoulders of his gaberdine coat were waterlogged with rain. He never drove a car where he could walk. 'You didn't tell me the Postmaster was under report for driving through a red light, having an out-of-date licence and no MoT certificate,' he complained. 'It helped a lot. He said "No" three times and meant it.' He handed Rogers a square of paper. 'I had to butter up the Exchange Supervisor and she's an old dear with breath like a blow torch.'

'I'll recommend you for a Queen's Police Medal,' Rogers promised him. 'Many have got it for less.'

He read the notes made by Coltart and they jolted him.

22430. Vosper, Vosper, Carradine & Galbraith, Solicitors, High Street.

24319. Lt. Col. Rodney Jagger, DSO, MBE, MC., Dormers, Castle Road.

21206. James Hacker, 21 Regent Crescent.

23222. Sir Andrew Adrian Wallace, JP., Spye Green Hall, High Moor.

31881. The Sun & Evening Echo, Commercial Street.

33764. Waldo Cecil Norton, Goshawk House, Spye Green.

21618. Harry Edmund Quint, The Old Rectory, Spaniards Rise.

It wasn't difficult for Rogers to identify 'PG' as Philip Galbraith of the legal firm. He sucked in his breath. Not because he was particularly surprised but because he was a friend of the Chief Constable's. 'DG' he guessed to be Donald Garwood, assistant editor of the highly moralistic *Sun & Evening Echo*. He added the names in pencil. At first glance he thought there must be a rational explanation for the inclusion of Wallace's name. Then he wrinkled his forehead in vexation and told himself not to be so bloody simple.

To Coltart, he said, 'Good stuff, sergeant. You've made my day if not the Chief Constable's. God knows what he's going to say when he knows that Galbraith, plus one of our own magistrates and a DSO and MC colonel have all been hammering on Frail's door with £10 cheques in their sweaty hands.' He turned down the corners of his mouth. 'Probably blame me for not leaving well alone.'

Coltart, who had been standing patient and bulky and

steaming, said, 'I haven't finished, sir.' His green eyes were glinting his satisfaction. 'Young Lashley turned up some information with his first knock. A chap called Midgley – he lives in a flat somewhere above Frail's – says he saw her leave with a man in a Rolls-Royce at about nine last night.'

Rogers said 'Agh!' with satisfaction. 'He did? What about her own car?'

'I don't know. That's all Lashley said. He thought it important enough to telephone in and leave a message for you. Do you want me to see this Midgley?'

Rogers regarded the array of papers on his desk with dislike. 'No. I've collected a migraine sorting this lot out. I never was an armchair detective. I want some fresh air, even if it is wet and laced with carbon monoxide.'

He shrugged himself into his raincoat. The afternoon was dying in a drizzle of grey rain. 'Leave Midgley to me, sergeant. I'd like you to go to the laboratory and see what, if anything, they've turned up on the Mini Cooper in particular.'

Before he left the office, he underlined in ink the name Sir Andrew Adrian Wallace and the amount of £850. It was beginning to bother him, not fitting the general pattern, irking his sense of orderliness.

There were too many 'AW' entries to equate with a common interest in French postage stamps, even if – and Rogers couldn't believe they did – the passions of stamp collectors ran that high. His earthy mind rejected the improbability but decided to read up on the French *Classiques* before interviewing Wallace.

Getting into his car, he remembered Quint's wife Judith and the occasion she had driven him up on to the moors, intent on an open-air seduction. The nub of his recollection was that she had driven him there in an elderly Rolls-Royce.

6

For the third time that day, Rogers dismounted from his car in Queen Anne's Road and climbed the cement steps to the geranium-smelling porch. This time he thumbed the bell-push at the side of the typed card reading *Martin Midgley Esq.*, *No. 3*, opening the door to the common entrance and stepping inside.

The door to Nancy Frail's flat was now securely locked; Rogers' signature, inked on a strip of tape stretching from door post to stile and fastened by thumb-impressed seals, forbidding admission.

The little man who limped down the stairs to greet Rogers was in the grey fifties with prominent thyroidic eyeballs. His scalp shone pink and hairless. His limp moustache was yellow-fringed with vaporized nicotine tars. The detective could smell the staleness of tobacco smoke on his clothing as they shook hands.

'Midgley,' the little man said in a soft limp voice. 'You are?'

'Rogers. Detective Chief Inspector Rogers.'

Midgley rubbed his palms together making a slithery sound. 'Come on up, chief inspector.'

Following him up the stairs, Rogers saw that he was club-footed.

His flat smelled of confined tobacco smoke and peppermint. His wife (a mountainous and pallid hybrid between a frog and a pekinese bitch, Rogers thought) sat on a blue satin settee, eating violet-sugared peppermint creams from a bulging paper bag. A cigarette smoked in an overflowing glass ashtray at her side. She was provisioned for an evening's hard reading with an opened box of chocolates, a drum of Turkish Delight, a twenty-packet of Players No. 6 cigarettes and several paperback books. Her fingers, pale magenta-tipped slugs, pushed creams into her tiny cupid's-bow mouth. Her eyes were cold blue; more frog than pekinese. They pinned Rogers with an unwinking sexless stare, taking in his raincoated bulk and swarthy maleness, but not letting it divert her from masticating. She remained hulked on the settee, her dropsical legs tucked beneath her. Rogers tried to visualize her *in coitus* with her little bald husband and failed.

There was a table at one end of the room stacked with account books and invoice files. 'I'm an accountant, chief inspector,' Midgley said, noticing Rogers' glance at them, 'and unfortunately I find it necessary to bring work home.'

Refusing a sherry, Rogers sat and smiled encouragingly at them both. He wasted his time with the fat woman but Midgley responded, the eternal little man basking in his warming moment of importance.

Rogers said, 'I understand you saw Miss Frail last night, Mr Midgley.'

He clucked. 'A sad business, chief inspector.' He glanced sideways at his wife. She was reading, her jowls bulging, seemingly a world away. 'A very popular young lady with, er, lots of friends.'

'So I understand,' Rogers said blandly, accepting the euphemism. 'You saw one of them last night?'

'Yes. About nine o'clock,' he said eagerly. 'I was looking out the window to check the weather. I happened to see a big black car down below, further along the road. I recognized it as a Rolls-Royce. There aren't many of those about. Even around here.' He made Queen Anne's Road seem the equivalent of Park Lane, W.1. 'Nobody got out immediately and that alone made me wonder.' He looked at his wife. 'Didn't it, dear?'

She nodded indifferently, the rolls of fat under her chin flopping.

He continued. 'Then a man got out from the driver's side of the car.' He waited.

'All right,' Rogers said. 'You knew him?'

'Not by name but he'd called on Miss Frail on a number of previous occasions. He'd blond or white hair, a slim figure.'

'Age?'

'Oh, fiftyish, although I never saw him in daylight.'

The description fitted Quint sufficiently for Rogers. His use of a Rolls-Royce added weight to it.

Midgley's pouched eyes fixed on Rogers', making his next remark significant. 'I rarely saw her friends in the daytime, chief inspector. And they always left their cars at the end of the road.'

Rogers defused the innuendo with irony. 'They probably didn't want to cause an obstruction, Mr Midgley. You are on a slight curve here. What happened after the man got out?'

'He came up the steps and, I presume, went inside Miss Frail's flat. I left the window then, not expecting his departure until at least the . . . the, er, small hours.'

Rogers' face was impassive against the revelations of this nosy little sod. There was one in every road thank God, he thought. 'And then?' he asked.

'After about five minutes I heard the car door banged and I looked out again. I saw the Rolls being driven away. When it passed under the road lamp opposite I saw Miss Frail in the passenger seat.' He lit a fresh cigarette direct from the stub of the old one.

'Good,' Rogers said. 'What was she dressed in?'

Midgley lifted his eyebrows. 'Oh, it was too dark for me to see that, chief inspector.'

'But not too dark to recognize her?'

Midgley peered at him as if doubtful whether he was a friend or an enemy. 'Well, I didn't actually see her . . . I

mean, it must have been her . . . his having just come . . .'
His voice withered under the frost of his wife's regard.

'But you did see her features?' Rogers persisted.

He was crestfallen. 'I must be frank,' he said bravely. 'I only assumed it was Miss Frail. Wasn't it?'

'I don't know, Mr Midgley,' Rogers said. 'You may be right. But I have to know just how sure you believe you are.'

'Well, after what you've said, not very.'

'He should be,' the fat woman surprisingly interjected, her voice glutinous around the bolus of chocolate cream in her mouth. She spoke as if Midgley wasn't there. 'He knows her well enough.' An unspoken *dirty little sod* hung in the air.

The accountant smiled like a kicked dog but for a microsecond there was murder in his eyes. Rogers didn't miss it and he thought that one day Midgley might find the courage to poison his vicious wife with a nasty caustic like oxalic acid that hurt both being swallowed and vomited back up.

'Oh?' he said politely.

'It's nothing, chief inspector,' Midgley said hastily. 'My wife is joking. A professional relationship only. I occasionally advise on buying and selling – particularly selling . . .' He cackled as if he'd said something clever. '. . . on the Exchange.'

'He spoke to her last night,' she said flatly over her open book, admitting of no argument.

Midgley swallowed. 'On the way in . . . coming back from a walk.' He had flushed a bright red on his naked scalp and was agonizingly embarrassed. 'We discussed the weather . . .'

The woman's 'h'm' was barely to be heard but it reached their ears like a small black malevolent moth.

'What time was this, Mr Midgley?' Rogers smiled at

him, recognizing a sexually frustrated bitch when he saw one and happy to help the little man along.

'Just before six.' He hesitated, then bit at his bottom lip. 'She was . . . oh, it couldn't be important.'

'Let me be the judge.'

Midgley glanced sideways at his wife. She was coughing on a cigarette, her face dangerously crimson, her eyes bulging. 'I'm not sure you'd want to know,' he said. 'I mean, it could be completely innocent. I wouldn't want to blacken a man's character . . .'

Realization came to Rogers. 'I see. You're trying to say I know the man?'

'Yes. You do know?'

'You tell *me*, Mr Midgley.'

'He was on his way out.' His eyes shifted. 'When he'd gone I naturally stopped and passed the time of the day with her.'

Rogers searched his face. 'There's more to it than that,' he said.

Again Midgley glanced at his wife. 'He was angry. She wasn't but he was.'

'In what way?'

'White-faced angry . . . bitter. As if he'd lost a quarrel with her.' He spoke as a man with some experience of losing quarrels. 'Miss Frail was quite calm, I thought. Not particularly caring. She acted as if nothing had happened. But that, of course,' he said, 'may have been her good manners.'

'You know the man's name?'

'Mr Lingard. He left in his green Bentley. He was about the only man who ever parked outside the house.'

'You know the names of the others?'

Before he could answer, the woman slapped her book down. Rogers read its title, *Sweet Heartbreak*, upside down, not being surprised. 'No, he doesn't,' she snapped. 'He isn't interested enough.' She dared her husband to say differently.

Rogers ignored her. 'Do you, Mr Midgley?'

The eyes meeting his apologized briefly for his cowardice. 'I know of no others, chief inspector,' he said. He indicated the piles of ledgers. 'My evenings are usually so occupied.'

'Where did Miss Frail garage her car?'

'In the next road. Number twenty-five St Marks.'

'You have a car?'

He shook his head and his dentures clacked. 'No. I've never felt the need.'

He held out his hand when Rogers left and the detective shook it. It lay in his fingers like a lump of damp fungus.

'You might fool *him*,' the woman said when they heard the door downstairs shut, 'but not me, you dirty-minded lecherous pig. You can't keep your filthy paws off anyone.'

Her spiteful tirade flowed unregarded beneath the level of his awareness as he lit his fifty-sixth cigarette of the day and turned the pages of a Sales Ledger. When she finally stopped and opened the drum of Turkish Delight he was as indifferent to the glutinous chewing as he had been to her noisy malignancy.

Before calling on Quint, Rogers returned to his office. There was a message form from Coltart on the blotting pad.

Sir,   *13th October.*
Preliminary Lab. Report.
1 Stone dust identified weathered fine-grain sandstone.
2 Lipstick on Gauloises cigs. similar lipsticks from flat and deceased's handbag.

3 *Black head hair with living root bulb found in deceased's clothing. Report will say minus 0.4 medulla; 93mm long with nodule suggesting hair cut approx. eight days previously.*

4 *Result of oestrogen and other checks on blood/ stomach contents unavailable for further three days.*

5 *Exterior of car definitely wiped clean of marks.*

(sgd) E. Coltart, D/Sergt. 7.50 p.m.

Rogers put it away in the drawer with the other case papers. Then he pulled the telephone handset towards him and dialled the Chief Constable's office code. He let it ring for a few seconds before shutting down. He hadn't expected him to be there but he had to know. Then he dialled the number of his home, hoping with his fingers crossed that he wouldn't be there either. When there was no answer he made a note of the time he had tried to contact him. He was pleased he wasn't to be deflected from his purpose either by any immediate considerations of the status of some of the names taken from Nancy Frail's diary or by Huggett's downgrading of the importance of the enquiry.

The Old Rectory at Spaniards Rise appeared as arrogantly shabby as he remembered it from his previous visits some four months previously. The iron gates, crooked on their stone columns, were, perhaps, rustier. The drive was certainly more lumpy with moss, the laurels a shade more unkempt.

Although the house was in total darkness, Rogers pulled hard at the cold iron ring of the bell-pull, hearing it clanking behind, it seemed, a dozen closed doors. When there was no answer he depressed the handle and pushed. The door remained solid and unmoving. He walked along the gravel to the rear of the house, shining the beam of his torch into the huge octagonal conservatory taking up the side of the house. Once it had been heated and lush with tropical plants; colourful with exotic birds and lizards and swarming insects; a miniature Borneo jungle for Quint's amusement and a nostalgic reminder of his service in the Fallic Islands.

It was now cold with broken panes of glass in the structure, the trees and plants no longer plump and glossy, their succulence wrinkled and blackened by an unheated English autumn. There were no birds in the drab foliage and nothing moved under the probing ray of the detective's torch. The small pond by which he and Judith Quint had so nearly copulated was dry and empty of its one-time colony of frogs. There was desolation about its memories and Rogers shivered.

An old stable in a cobbled yard at the rear, obviously used as a garage, was empty.

Rogers looked at his watch. It was 8.40 and he had time to see Dominis before his appointment with Bridget. The thought of her was a warming ball of fire in his stomach.

Broken Cross was a rectangle of ferociously-shaved turf with a few silver birch trees clumped in its centre. Around the perimeter were clapboard, split-level chalet houses with too many windows and glass doors for civilized living.

He saw the window curtains of No. 18 being pulled aside as he slammed the door of his car.

She opened the glass and wrought-iron door a scant six inches before he could knock, peering at him through the crack. He saw a girl with long straight yellow hair, a disintegrating rope espadrille on the one foot visible to him and a floral smock that had surrendered any attempt at minimizing the huge paunch of her pregnancy. Very pregnant women made Rogers nervous. He always feared being required to cope with a messily premature birth.

She shivered in the cold night air. 'Are you the police?'

67

'Yes. Detective Chief Inspector Rogers,' he answered. 'Mrs Dominis?'

'Come in.' She was apparently satisfied he would not rape her. 'Have you found him?'

Inside, he studied her. She wore no lipstick; no anything on her formless face. She was pretty but not attractive; making, nevertheless, a pleasant change from the grotesquery of Midgley's wife. Her huge bloated belly made her unstockinged legs look spindly.

He didn't much like the house. There seemed square metres of uncarpeted, comfortless space only sparsely furnished with plastic chairs and metal tables. The walls were of natural pinewood, the spiral stairs of iron. There would be a Sauna bath somewhere up there. Rogers had felt more at home in his dentist's waiting-room.

He sat in a chair shaped like a surrealist motor tyre. It gripped his buttocks with a giant's warm hand. He looked around for ashtrays. There were none so he kept his pipe unlit in his fingers.

'Have we found who?' he asked, settling himself.

'My husband, of course. Isn't that why you're here?'

'I came to see Mr Dominis, if that's what you mean,' he said carefully. 'You say he's missing?'

She stared at him. 'Shouldn't you know?'

'Not necessarily,' he said testily. 'I am CID. Details of missing people come to me fortuitously or only when there appears some good reason why they should. May I use your telephone to check?'

She nodded. He extracted his buttocks from the almost human grip of the chair and went to the telephone in the hall.

'There's a completed form in your IN tray,' the Information Room Inspector told him incisively. 'I put it there myself this morning at three o'clock. When you were still in bed.'

68

Rogers swallowed his momentary ill-humour. Park Dominis wouldn't have meant anything to him either at that time. 'Tell me about it,' he said. 'I didn't get round to sorting through my trays today.'

'Park Dominis, Flight Captain with Concordant-Global Airways. Reported by his wife, Mrs Philippa Dominis of 18 Broken Cross at 2.05 a.m. today. Missing since he left his home in his car at 7.30 p.m. Said he was going out for a drink. Dress: dark blue lightweight coat, a buff pullover, light blue linen trousers and soft shoes.' He gave the missing pilot's personal description which tallied with that already known to Rogers. 'It says here,' the Inspector continued, 'there's no known reason for his absence: job secure, good health, financially stable, no domestic troubles other than his wife's expecting a child in three weeks time. We've made a check at Blakehill Airfield: no help there. He's not flying again until tomorrow so they aren't concerned. Not yet. His description's circulated with the number of his car. We last checked with Mrs Dominis at six this evening when he hadn't returned home.'

'Good.' Rogers knew this had been well handled for what it appeared. Hundreds of persons went missing each year from the area; some for days, some for ever. Only a very few warranted special action. He lowered his voice. 'Recirculate it for special attention. On my authorization. Any results direct to me, please.'

'What about Mr Lingard?'

'What about him?'

'He's had his copy of the Missing Persons Form. Will he want to know of any progress?'

Rogers thought that one out. 'You don't know?'

'I'm sorry. What don't I know?'

'I can't imagine it's much of a secret. He's resigned.'

'That's a shaker ...'

'Don't discuss it,' Rogers said brusquely. 'Nobody's very happy about it. Just leave the Dominis matter with me. And dig Sergeant Coltart out from wherever he is. I want to see him in my office in half-an-hour's time.'

He replaced the receiver and returned to the woman. She was standing, waiting.

'I've got the picture,' he said. 'I'm sorry.'

Her fingers twined together in her agitation. 'He's not been found?'

He shook his head. 'You've no idea why he should stay away so long?'

Her eyes dropped from his. 'No.' Then she said, puzzled, 'You said you wanted to speak to him. Can you tell me why?'

'I wanted some information from him.' His face was wooden, not revealing anything. 'You are his second wife?'

She clutched at the mound of her belly and sat abruptly. 'No,' she said. 'But you knew that already, didn't you?'

'Yes.'

'We live together because we can't get married. Not until Park can get a divorce from that poisonous bitch of a woman.'

'You mean Nancy Frail?'

'That's what she calls herself, thank God.' She looked sad. 'Will Park get into trouble, Mr Rogers? With his company, I mean.'

'I shouldn't think so. Not unless it affects his flying.' He grinned companionably at her.

'Did *she* send you?'

'I'm here because of her.'

Her forehead wrinkled. 'There's something wrong, isn't there? Because you're here looking for him. Not even knowing he's missing.' She hesitated. 'Is it about the stamps?'

70

Rogers' memory produced a mental picture of the newspaper clipping and Wallace's letter. 'The French Louis Napoleons?' he countered, fitting himself back into the embrace of the plastic chair.

'You *know*!' she cried despairingly. 'She told you.' She cracked her knuckles in her anguish. 'She had everything of his. Including the stamps. It was the first time he'd ever bought anything that turned out to have been stolen and she had to find out.'

He nodded as if he knew everything.

'He would have owned up when he found out because he hadn't known. But he'd brought them through Customs in his Flight Bag and that would have cost him his job.' She bit her bottom lip hard. 'Smuggling. It wasn't really. She said she'd report it to the police if he tried to get them back. Such stupid little bits of coloured paper,' she said sadly, 'to cause so much trouble.'

'So are bank notes,' Rogers said. 'Little bits of paper, I mean. Is that where he went last night? To her flat?'

'Yes,' she whispered, bowing her head, the hair falling about her face like yellow curtains. 'He was watching her. Trying to get evidence for a divorce. He wants it so desperately he was even willing to risk her saying something about the stamps. He's been watching her off and on for weeks. When he has the opportunity; which isn't very often with so many night charter flights.' She flicked her hair back with a shake of her head. 'She's a filthy little cow, you know. And clever with it. She's blackmailing Park, Mr Rogers.'

'She is?'

'Yes. She sucks a hundred pounds separation allowance from him every month. For bloody dam' all.' Her blue eyes sparkled with the first showing of real spirit. 'Park never deserved a bitch like her.'

'He definitely said he intended watching her last night?'

'Yes. He doesn't otherwise go out.'

'Always at her flat?'

'Mostly, but sometimes he's had to follow her to other places.' She clenched her hands into small fists. 'All this time and he's never *seen* anything. Nothing he can use . . .'

'Do you know the men she was meeting?'

She was wary, pulling a strand of hair across her face and holding it between her lips. 'No.'

'But he mentioned names?'

'Is any of this going to hurt Park?'

He stared at her. 'You should be the best judge of that.'

'Park isn't a criminal, Mr Rogers,' she said earnestly.

'All right, I'll accept that. Now tell me about the men.'

'He thought one was her optician. A man called Hacker. She stayed with him all one night. I remember that because he didn't come home until dawn. Then there's Gal . . . Galbraith I believe it is. A lawyer.' She laughed without humour. 'He handled the separation proceedings for her and got Park to agree to paying her all that money. He should have fought it but he didn't want it splashed in the newspapers. It doesn't seem right, does it? Her own lawyer . . .'

'Go on,' Rogers said patiently.

'There was a man living in a big house at Spye Green. She's been there a lot, Park says.' She searched her recollection. 'There's a man who flies hawks and a man with a very old green car. A veteran model, Park called it. Oh dear,' she said, 'I've such a wretched memory and it's all so beastly and squalid.'

'Life usually is,' he assured her. 'Was there a man with a Rolls-Royce?'

'Yes, there was. His name was Qu . . . Quill . . . ? Something beginning with a Q.'

'Quint?'

'That's it,' she said. The flesh tightened over her cheekbones. 'You know all this, don't you? Like you knew about me.'

'I know a little.' He shrugged deprecatingly. 'I can never know too much. Is there anything else?'

'Park thought she knew he was watching her. It wasn't anything he was very good at. She was so horrible in her promiscuity I don't expect she cared.'

'I don't think you need worry about her any more,' he said casually, but watching her closely. 'She's dead.'

Her hand flew to her mouth. 'Oh, dear God! Not by Park! What have I done! What have I said!' Her eyes rolled from side to side.

'Don't distress yourself,' Rogers said calmly. 'She died of natural causes. Of a coronary thrombosis.'

She was silent for a long time, retrieving the fragments of her lost composure. Then she said, 'That wasn't fair of you. You could have told me before.'

'I could. But I didn't.'

She gave him an unhappy smile. 'I'm sorry. You have your job to do and you must do it as you think best. You know,' she said, tightening her mouth, 'I can't say I'm sorry because I'm not. I'm even glad. But where's Park if she's dead? That's what I have to know.' She held her belly again. 'I'm frightened, Mr Rogers. Things are happening . . .'

'Such as?'

'I had a telephone call earlier on. About two hours ago. A man asked for Park.'

'Just like that?'

'No. "Mr Dominis", he said. I thought he was a policeman. When I told him he hadn't returned he shut down on me. When the inspector telephoned at six, I asked him. He said they hadn't called before. It worried me . . . here on my own . . .'

'Don't let it,' he reassured her. 'I'm sure there'll be a

73

simple answer to all of it.' But the little comfort he gave her was illusory. When he found him, Rogers would require Dominis to answer some uncomfortable questions.

'Does he smoke?' he asked.

'No, never.' Her nose wrinkled her disgust and Rogers was glad he had kept his pipe unlit in his hand. Dominis could, of course, be a secret smoker in the toilet but he didn't think so.

'An odd question, Mrs Dominis, but it might prove useful. Do you know when your husband had his hair cut?'

Although perplexed, she was grateful to him for his courtesy in addressing her as Dominis's wife. And it kept her talking. 'It is an odd question, Mr Rogers.'

'Please answer it,' he said, smiling. 'It really could help.'

'About a week ago. I did it myself.'

'Have you a photograph I could use?'

She produced one from the drawer of a scarlet-painted sideboard.

It showed Dominis in his Airways uniform. He was a handsome, rakish man with a lecher's narrow moustache and eyes a woman would be a fool to trust. Rogers thought he must have been tamed considerably since the photograph was taken.

In the hall he saw the missing man's dark blue cap with its shiny braided peak and the gilt winged badge with a C-GA motif. 'May I?' he asked, taking it from its peg. There were a number of hairs inside adhering to the plastic lining. Unobserved, he slid one out. Later he would put it between two unused pages of his notebook.

He hesitated as he left the house. 'Get someone to stay with you,' he urged. He looked at her swollen figure. 'I'll let you know as soon as I get some news.'

7

Rogers made a hurried return to Spaniards Rise, flogging a hot engine up the steep hill leading to it. On the way he had been blinded by the undipped plate-sized headlights of an approaching car. As it passed him he had had a momentary glimpse of a brass radiator shell and glittering exhaust pipes sprouting from a long green bonnet. It could only have been Lingard's Bentley.

The house was still in darkness and Quint had not returned. The wheels of Rogers' car left furrows in the gravel and moss as he took off in a mood of frustrated irritation.

Coltart was in his office waiting his return, his jaws bulging on a wooden toothpick.

'Did I drag you away from television, sergeant?' Rogers asked, knowing he never watched it. He was in the mood to quarrel with someone.

'No,' Coltart replied mildly. 'You had me pulled out of The Saracen's Head.'

'They must miss you,' Rogers said ungraciously.

'Mr Lingard might. He was there earlier on.' Coltart's bull mastiff face was expressionless.

Rogers thinned his lips. 'I want to see him.'

'You should choose some other time.'

'Oh?'

Coltart didn't like Lingard: had liked him even less since he had learned of his resignation. But he was still reluctant. 'He was knocking back Pernods like milk shakes. And not being what I'd call gregarious.'

'Be explicit, sergeant.' Rogers was frowning.

'All right. He was nasty-drunk. Ready to hang one on

75

the barman's chin if he so much as coughed for the wrong reason.' Coltart bit hard on the toothpick, blinking his eyes. He might have wanted it to happen.

Rogers checked his watch. It was nine thirty-five. He had wasted time returning to Spaniards Rise. 'What time did he leave?'

'About nine.' His face was serious. 'In the mood he was, he's probably tearing some poor bastard's arm off at this very moment.'

'He's cutting his losses, sergeant, rationalizing his gullibility. We all do it in different ways.'

That was difficult for Coltart to understand and he shrugged Lingard and his problems away.

Rogers abruptly discarded the subject of his former second-in-command. 'I want some urgent background information. Tonight if possible. And I'm sure it is. Dig out the Area and Beat constables concerned. Check Vehicles and Firearms records, anything you can think of that will provide useful facts.' He ticked off names on a list with his pencil. 'A complete rundown on Jagger, Hacker, Wallace, Garwood and Norton. I know enough about Galbraith and Quint to be getting on with. See me at eight-thirty in the morning and brief me on their domestic set-ups, what they do to scratch a living, what cars they run, their general reputations. That sort of thing.' He gave the sergeant the photograph of Dominis. 'Get Sergeant Lucas to run off a dozen copies of this. Tonight. It's Exhibit A, Nancy Frail's missing husband. It's too bloody convenient she should die just when he so badly wanted a divorce. More than significant that he's coincidentally vanished.'

It was pure Coltart that he made no comment about Rogers' giving him a full night's work. 'Shall I telephone you if I get anything really useful?'

Rogers kept his expression straight. 'I hope to be off the

air for an hour or two. Leave any message with the Information Room Inspector.'

When Coltart had lumbered from the office, he lifted the telephone receiver and dialled the number of St Jude's Hospital. The operator finally located Bridget in the pathological laboratory.

'Still working, Bridget?' he said lightly. 'I thought you'd be polishing sherry glasses.'

'At the moment I'm working overtime, finishing off the staining of some interesting little wrigglers for you.'

'That sounds fine. I rang to say your visitor is likely to be about twenty minutes overdue. Does it matter?'

Her voice was neutral. 'I shall be here in the lab.' Which left Rogers wondering and he chewed his lip uneasily.

He next dialled the Chief Constable's home number. He was in, sounding distended with someone else's dinner.

'I telephoned earlier, sir,' Rogers said. 'You told me to keep in touch.' He gave him the lot, including his interviews with Midgley and the woman calling herself Mrs Dominis. Telling him thus made it seem as if he had been digging into a sewer. Which he knew would upset Huggett's rather prissy, unworldly views on the nature of humanity.

Huggett found his voice. 'You're certain of all this?'

'Most of it. Not all. It's the general picture I've got.'

'I can't believe it,' he said flatly. 'Not Sir Andrew . . . Mr Galbraith: this Lieutenant Colonel . . . you *must* be mistaken. People like that don't do those sort of things.'

Rogers was irritated that Huggett's snobbery equated professional and social position with a strict sexual morality. 'With respect,' he said bluntly, 'I fail to see why not. You don't have to be an unwashed illiterate to fornicate with a whore. I'll quote some national names if I have to,' he added helpfully, sailing very close to the wind of insolence.

'Thank you, Mr Rogers,' Huggett said frostily. 'I am well aware of the point you are trying to make. I meant these particular men. I am equally aware that it could be none of our business. I still believe you may be mistaken.'

Rogers said patiently, 'I concede that Sir Andrew's cheque may have been for the purchase of the French stamps. But those, being apparently stolen, certainly need investigation. Nor does their purchase explain Miss Frail's three visits to his house. Or his five to hers.'

'Visits to his house? To hers?'

'I'll admit they could have stayed at an hotel but that would be dangerous. I believe the bracketed "h"s and "a"s after each set of initials indicate Home and Away visits.' He laughed briefly. 'She seemed to have had a sense of humour, whatever else.'

The noise Huggett made was indicative of a vast disbelief.

'I could be wrong,' Rogers admitted, 'but it fits. Anyway – leaving Wallace aside for a moment – the other payments need explaining. And, as an important corollary, the matter of who dumped her body in the lane. She may not even have been dead. Which would aggravate the offence considerably.'

'I don't like it, Mr Rogers.'

'Neither do I, sir,' Rogers answered, wilfully misunderstanding him. 'It smells like a privy to me. One of the old-fashioned kind.'

'When I say I don't like it, I mean I don't like our getting so involved in what appears to be a moral issue.'

Rogers scowled into the mouthpiece. 'You know already, sir,' he said patiently, 'I'm not concerned with any moral issue. I'm concerned with one fact only. Who had sexual intercourse with her before – or while – she died. Not why. Anyway, we're already involved. I've the Pathological Laboratory working on it. I've sent exhibits to the Forensic Science Laboratory and I've made the enquiries I've already mentioned.' Before Huggett could object again, he continued, 'There are also the other matters I've mentioned. Dominis hasn't gone missing for nothing. The woman he's living with is about nine-and-a half months pregnant and he isn't going to default on a highly paid job with C-GA for a triviality. Stretching a point, Quint's missing from his home too. Why he called at Miss Frail's flat is something only he can answer.'

'I don't quarrel with any of that,' Huggett said stiffly. He was liking it less and less and it sounded in the tone of his voice. He was also having to concede points to Rogers' argument. 'But I insist we cannot afford a profitless scandal involving public figures.'

'We'll have one anyway,' Rogers promised him stubbornly, 'if I don't get to these people before Lingard does. He's got it into his head Frail was raped and he's in the mood to do something bloody-minded about it. I believe he's already looking for Dominis and Quint. He won't miss out on the others either.'

'You must stop him.'

Rogers allowed his exasperation to sound. 'If I may say so, that's easier said than done. Neither of us has any effective authority over him.'

'He is still a police officer and subject to my instructions.'

Oh God! Rogers groaned to himself. Aloud, he said, 'And he's liable to tell us . . . me, anyway . . . to get stuffed. He knows there's nothing to stop him from asking questions, making what enquiries he chooses as a private citizen. Unless he actually obstructs my own enquiries I can't touch him.'

'And that's that,' he growled as he replaced the receiver after several minutes more of querulous doubts from Huggett. He would be exposed and naked to disciplinary trouble if there was no more in the investigation than a simple coronary thrombosis and a reasonable explanation from somebody to account for her being where she had been found. It was a sobering thought but he wasn't going to allow it to give him an ulcer.

Before he left the office he swallowed a whisky, washing and scrubbing his teeth in the cloakroom at the end of the corridor. He scowled at his face in the mirror; shadowless and clear-etched under the unflattering strip lighting. 'You bloody lecher,' he mouthed at it. 'You should know better.'

In the car he shaved his whiskers as he drove, holding the steering-wheel rim in one fist. He afterwards smoothed his chin and jowls with the back of his hand, checking he'd made an acceptable job of it.

Bridget, trim in a grey woollen dress, was alone in the laboratory, writing notes.

She smiled at him on his entry. An easy, friendly smile that said nothing at all. 'A positive on the semen test,' she greeted him without preamble. 'All the spermatozoa you'll ever need. Your girl-friend was carnally known, possibly during or immediately prior to her coronary. An over-excited orgasm, I expect,' she murmured drily.

Rogers turned down the corners of his mouth. 'It's a sobering thought,' he said. 'To drop dead *in situ*, I mean. More particularly if either you or your partner isn't supposed to be where it happens.'

Bridget remarked calmly, 'If the need ever arises, I'll take my partner's blood pressure first.' She said it as if the circumstance was highly improbable and Rogers had a depressing moment of doubt.

She stood and moved to a bench, removing a glass box cover from a binocular microscope. She peered into the eyepieces and adjusted the slide stage with the twist of a gear wheel. She flicked a light switch and moved back, saying, 'Have a look, George. I'm pleased with them.'

Three violet whip-tailed tadpoles wobbled into his field of vision. They were lifeless and unmoving. 'Why violet?' he asked. 'The last time I saw any, they were cobalt.'

'I used Biebrich scarlet and methylene-blue,' she said. 'It's the Van Gogh factor in me coming out. Next time they might be emerald.'

'How many are you going to need to allow you to stand in the witness box and prove intercourse?'

'One. Out of, perhaps, the five million in a single ejaculation.'

'Bless my soul. And you found only three?' He was sardonic.

'Idiot! These are in the thinnest film from a wrung-out swab. Anyway, three lovely little fellows like that will be sufficient to prove sexual intercourse for you. And each only about point o-five of a millimetre long.'

'But not identifiable to any particular man,' he said glumly.

'Not unless you'd like to wait a few years while I rear one in a test tube.' Much of what they were saying was nonsense, a camouflage for their need: Rogers', clear-cut and unambiguous; hers, shallow-rooted and very much at the mercy of chance emotional currents.

She replaced the glass box over the microscope. 'Are you happy now?'

'I'm thirsty.'

Her eyes were dark orange as she regarded him coolly, baiting him. 'Oh, yes. I asked you up for a sherry, didn't I.' She snapped off the lights. 'You'd better come on up.'

Her apartment was on the top floor of the annexe. In the lift they were unspeaking and preoccupied. Rogers felt his visit had developed into a cold-blooded assignation and he fretted to say something. There was nothing that wouldn't be banal and he remained silent.

She slipped the catch on the inside of the door. It was a warm, lived-in place with cushioned furniture and small thickets of potted plants climbing ceilingwards. Through an arch, its curtain undrawn, he could see her bed. There was no way of his knowing whether he was meant to. There were books everywhere and the wired-together bones of a spinal column occupied a place on a coffee table. He shed his overcoat and dropped it in an easy chair already containing Moritz's *Pathology of Trauma* and a fat textbook on bacteriology.

While she poured sherry at a trolley he went to her. She stopped, one glass filled, the bottle poised, her eyes questioning him over her shoulder. There was a shadow of mockery in them. 'No *hors-d'œuvre* after all, George?' She put the bottle down and faced him.

He put his impatient hands on her waist and pulled her to him. His need for her was urgent, almost brutal, and she felt it.

Her hands were flat on his chest, pushing him back. 'The last time you were here, George, you had objections. You considered loving me inconsistent with your status as a police officer. Or something,' she added.

He kissed the tip of her nose. 'I must have been mad.' He was drunk with wanting her.

'You were,' she agreed coolly. 'Had you considered that it is *I* who might now have objections?'

He released her abruptly, his expression angry. 'I'm sorry,' he said slowly. He turned and picked the bottle from the trolley with a shaking hand, splashing sherry into the empty glass. 'So I've made a bloody idiot of myself. I'll drink your sherry and leave you to it.' He banged the bottle down.

She reached for her own sherry and drained the glass. Then she laughed in his face. 'You've taken a lot for granted, Detective Chief Inspector Rogers,' she taunted him. 'Did you expect me to unzip myself and fall flat on my back?'

There was only one thing he could say and he said it. Coldly and definitely. 'As a matter of fact, I did.'

They stared at each other for long seconds. Then she said softly, 'How wrong can you be, George?' She moistened her lips with her tongue and turned her back to him. '*You* unzip me.'

He hesitated. His tongue was thick in his mouth. 'You aggravating bitch. Did that make you feel better?'

'Yes. Sadism becomes me.'

There was a spattering of tealeaf freckles on her glossy shoulders as he unpeeled the dress from her. She twisted in his arms and bit him hard on the throat, making him flinch. 'Watch it,' she said, her mouth hot on his flesh. 'I could also be a were-pathologist with a Dracula syndrome.' Her hands were pulling at his shirt front.

On the bed, her palms pressing on his shoulder-blades, she whispered, 'No. You needn't be *that* old-fashioned, poppet. You can't make me pregnant. It's one of the unadvertised emoluments of the medical profession.'

When they had each expended their stored-up lusts on the other, they lay side by side, their warm flanks touching. She ran a fingernail from the point of his chin, down the median line of his chest, along his flat belly to the genitals and kept it there.

'If I ever get you on the table, George,' she murmured, 'I'll bottle it in formalin and label it *Un Spécimen Formidable*. It would look lovely in the laboratory. In time,' she added drowsily, 'I could make a definitive collection of them . . .'

'You flatter me,' he grunted, 'and for God's sake don't say things like that. Not even in fun.'

When he left Bridget's apartment, Rogers was rubber-legged with fatigue and his neck ached. His conscience was an acid eating into his stomach. He felt that somehow he had been infected with the sexual aura of the death he was investigating and the dead woman's erotic shadow darkened his thinking. As he let himself in his front door he cursed himself for being old-maidish about it.

At four in the morning he awoke with a yell, then lay writhing and twisting with a black knot of worry in his gut. He suffered an enormity of guilt. Adultery was suddenly the ugliest word in the world. Stealing from the Force Imprest Account seemed by comparison a prosaic trifle. Although wishing futilely the night's happening could be undone he yet knew himself fallible enough for it to be repeated. That women were attracted to his cynical masculinity didn't help. He grimaced in the dark. Bridget had called him a yummy dish. He was in the mood to be Calvinistic in his interpretation of sexual morality and it was dawn before he rationalized his guilt and stuck a less ugly label on it.

8

Waiting for Coltart in his office, Rogers thought he had made too much of the episode with Bridget. But the stump of his conscience was still there, nagging at him in a minor key. Even Joanne's stiff-necked obstinacy and a sullen breakfast hadn't seemed reason enough to excuse his lechery of the night before.

Coltart arrived freshly showered and shaved. His eyes were clear and unpouched. He would, anyway, refuse to yawn on principle.

'Sit down, sergeant,' Rogers said. 'You've had some sleep?'

'A couple of hours in the office chair.'

'Good.' Rogers absently stuffed tobacco into his pipe. It was the first few grammes of the ounce he would smoke during the day. He reached over and switched on the tape recorder. Then he leaned back and said, 'Right. Fill me in.'

Coltart had his notes spread on his knees. 'I'd better start with the late Lieutenant Colonel Rodney Jagger,' he said.

Rogers raised his eyebrows and sat up. 'Late?' he echoed.

'On the eleventh of April he was grubbing out some hedge roots when he had a cerebral haemorrhage. He died in hospital next day. I checked with the coroner's officer. He's dead all right.'

Rogers scratched his name from the list. 'Dying, no doubt, in an odour of sanctity,' he remarked. 'In one way that'll please the Chief Constable. Better dead than damned.'

'Number two. James Hacker. Thirty and unmarried. An optician: Fellow of the British Opticians Association, Fellow of the Spectacle Makers Company. And a hell of a feller with the women. One of those, I'm told, who looks down their bosoms while he's fitting them with glasses.'

'Who wouldn't be an optician,' Rogers murmured. 'What does he look like? I only know of him.'

'Black hair, slim build, Mexican-type moustache. Wears glasses.'

'Do you know an optician who doesn't?'

Coltart considered that. 'Now you mention it, no. This one wears octagonals. A natty dresser and drives an open Porsche. He has a record of minor traffic offences. A very nice chap apparently and good at his job. Lives in a flat over the shop and parks his car in a lock-up behind.'

'Like you, sergeant,' Rogers observed. 'A bachelor with nothing to lose but his freedom.'

That bounced off Coltart's imperturbability. 'Number three. Sir Andrew Wallace.' He shrugged meaty shoulders. 'Deputy Chairman of the Bench. Conservative big wheel. Birthday Honours list knighthood two years ago for political services. Runs a small dairy farm out of town. You already know what he looks like. He's a widower, his wife dying ten years ago. His sister, Constance, looks after the house. She's unmarried, about thirty-five . . .'

'I know of her too. I'm told she keeps it snapped shut like an Old Age Pensioner's purse and likes her gin. Not a bad-looking woman either but a bit on the hefty side.'

'That wasn't quite my information,' Coltart said. 'There's rumour of a boy-friend she sees on the quiet.'

'I asked for gossip. I'm getting it.'

'Sir Andrew runs an old silver-coloured Daimler, she has a blue Austin. They have a woman, Mrs Jacobs, who goes in daily to dust the Rembrandts or whatever. They've money but not enough to spare for a yacht after keeping the house together. His grandfather was Lieutenant General "Khyber Pass" Napier Wallace whose worthy statue blocks the view from the Law Courts.'

Rogers looked glum. 'And Wallace himself the most excruciatingly respectable bore of them all. They all are,' he muttered, 'until they're found out. Just the cosy sort of man to ask if he's been sleeping with a whore. His only known vice, French *Classiques*.'

'Yes?' Coltart said politely and uncomprehendingly.

'Postage stamps,' Rogers explained, 'issued in the eighteen-fifties. Some of them worth a small fortune. I only know because I took five minutes off yesterday and checked at a stamp shop. There's one – a ten-centime bistre – valued at over £650. So a collection of them isn't pimply schoolboy stuff.'

If the big sergeant was impressed he didn't show it. 'Number four. Donald Garwood. Assistant editor of *The*

Sun & Evening Echo. You can cross him off your list too . . . I think. He fractured his ankle three weeks ago.'

'Falling out of the Frail bed, I expect.'

'No. Stepping off a kerb or something similar. Anyway, he's immobilized in plaster. Has to hobble about with a couple of sticks. I did learn something useful though. Miss Frail was a copy-taster with the *Echo* before she married Diminis.'

'When Garwood probably got it for nothing. All right. He can't drive a car so I've crossed him off. Who's next?'

'A nasty little man. Waldo Norton. A bone-idle bugger who flies hawks and screws anything that stands still long enough. He's kept by his wife who has some money of her own.'

'She must be soft,' Rogers said disparagingly.

'I think he keeps her fairly happy as well. He's the type, I'm told, who can jump on a woman's face and make her come back for more.'

'Don't ever try it, sergeant. He's a smaller man than you.' All this was minimizing Rogers' own peccadillo and he felt happier. He smiled at Coltart.

'He runs a dark green Citroën Safari with a white roof. Carries his birds in it too. He's a quick-tempered man with a mean streak in him. Fortyish, five-feet nothing with an oversized ego. He wears ginger Elizabethan whiskers and a velvet jacket.' That seemed to finish him completely so far as Coltart was concerned. 'I quote the local constable, "All wind and piss".'

'I've seen him about. And his car. He always has a skinny liver-and-white pointer bitch with him. Frail wasn't as choosey as I imagined.'

'I think he bathes regularly and smells all right,' Coltart said solemnly. 'It's just he's such a bouncy, arrogant little sod.' He put his notes in his pocket and yawned behind closed teeth.

Rogers saw it make the sergeant's eyes water. 'You'd better get some sleep,' he said sympathetically. 'The first thing this afternoon I want you to arrange for Midgley to make up a Photo-fit picture of the man he saw visiting the Frail flat. It was dark and he was thirty feet up but I bet he saw every pore in his skin.' He gave Coltart the hair he had taken from Dominis's flying cap. It lay coiled in a glassine envelope. 'Drop this in at the laboratory. Ask them to do a quick check of it against the hair they found in Frail's clothing.'

He read his watch. The Chief Constable normally arrived in his office at nine-thirty. If he wanted to avoid him – and he did – he would have to move fast. He made some brief telephone calls.

There was no answer from Quint's house and Dominis had not returned. Bridget was in the mortuary with a cirrhosis of the liver and unavailable.

He located Galbraith at his office. 'Yes, George?' he answered. 'What poor devil have you got inside this morning?'

Rogers cleared his throat. 'Nobody, Phil. They're all pleading guilty. An admirable attitude.' He waited a second. 'I'd like to speak to you myself.'

The solicitor sounded surprised. 'Of course, my dear chap. You're not in trouble?'

'No. I just want to speak to you, Phil.'

'This morning?'

'If I can.'

'It'll have to be soon. I'm due in court on a domestic in an hour.'

'Ten minutes, Phil.'

Constance Wallace answered his last call. 'Sir Andrew's on the farm,' she said. Although her words were formal, they sounded warm, her voice mellifluous. Rogers wondered how it had remained unsoured after thirty-five years of her being *virgo intacta*. 'He'll be back at eleven. Can I tell him what you want?'

There was an awkward pause. Rogers tapped his front teeth with the stem of his pipe. 'Strictly legal stuff,' he assured her cheerfully.

'Of course,' she said. 'You can't talk about it on the telephone.'

As he drove through the OUT gate, so Huggett entered through the IN. Rogers showed his teeth in the rear-view mirror. It had been a near thing. He had the day to himself now and things to do.

Galbraith rose from his overloaded desk and shook hands warmly, his round face ruddy with good living. He removed pink-taped bundles from a chair.

'Sit down, George. Nice to see you again.' His grey eyes told Rogers nothing. He was a short, barrel-chested man with a fruity voice. The smooth grey flannel suit he wore had been tailored to disguise an ambitious belly.

'Well,' he said comfortably, 'what can I do for you?' He lit a cigarette with an onyx desk lighter and smiled.

Rogers checked unsuccessfully for the microphone head concealed under a seemingly innocent newspaper or folder. He said, 'I came to see you about Nancy Frail, Phil,' leaving the words to hang in the air between them.

The cigarette jerked between Galbraith's fingers. A look of concern crossed his face. It didn't reach his eyes. 'I read about it in the *Echo* last night. How did she die?'

'Apparently quite naturally. Of a coronary thrombosis. She was found in her car.'

'Unbelievable.' He wagged his head sadly. 'She was a client of mine, George. I handled her separation.' He took a lungful of smoke. 'But why are *you* interested?' His eyes were veiled with wariness. 'I mean, if she died naturally . . .'

89

'She was taken to where she was found. Dumped there.'

'I see. That's not so good, is it.'

'No. I'm checking on her associates.' He didn't particularly like Galbraith but would get no pleasure from putting him through the wringer. There was a word for that sort of nastiness: *Schadenfreude*. It was absent from Rogers' make-up.

'You mean her professional and business contacts?'

'No. I mean her social contacts. You in particular.'

The thread of smoke from his cigarette zig-zagged like ribboned silk through a patch of bright sunlight above his head. 'I don't know what you're implying, George,' he said at last, a chill in his voice, 'but I think you should be careful. My connections with Miss Frail were entirely professional.'

'She kept a diary, Phil,' Rogers said casually.

The solicitor's ruddy face went pasty. Only the sound of the traffic outside could be heard in the quiet room. Then he forced out, 'A diary isn't evidence of anything or against anybody.' He didn't sound too confident.

'No, it might not be. But it could form the basis for some pretty searching enquiries.'

'I see. All right. Assuming Miss Frail made some notes, what do they amount to?'

Rogers produced his notebook and selected a page. 'They record your nine visits to her flat since the thirteenth of January, the last being on the first of this month.' He put the notebook back in his pocket and stood, moving away. 'If the answer's "no", Phil, I won't waste any more of your time.'

'But you wouldn't be leaving it at that?'

'No.'

'You're really going to dig for some dirt on this, aren't you.'

'I didn't put the dirt there. But the answer is yes, if I have to.'

'Sit down, George,' he said wearily. 'I don't suppose I'm the only married man to have had a mistress.'

'No. We all do what we can to spread it around.' It was as far as Rogers could go in acknowledging a common imperfection. In part, it was a confession. He returned to his chair.

Galbraith reached down and opened a drawer, taking out a brandy bottle. 'The good old therapeutic stand-by for uncovered sin,' he said with a chalky smile. He produced a small glass and poured a stiff dose into it. 'You can't, of course?'

'Not now, Phil. Are you going to tell me about it?'

Galbraith drank the brandy in one gulp. 'There isn't much to tell. I handled her legal affairs on her leaving her husband. We were attracted to each other and that was that. It happens all the time.'

'So it's nothing to get into a stew about.'

Galbraith measured Rogers with his wary eyes. 'How far does this go, George?'

'Not far if you aren't connected with her death. Or with the disposal of her body.'

'Well, I'm not. You know my wife, George.'

Rogers did. She was a sinewy, hacking-jacketed, hunting woman with a hardbitten face and a leather backside. She was older than her husband: the type to put him well down on the list of her affections. Certainly below her two horses and her dogs. As he remembered her, she wasn't likely to approve such a debilitating non-sport as sexual intercourse either with herself or anyone else.

'Yes,' he acknowledged, 'I do.'

'You know my partners.'

He knew them as well. Both active churchmen and as narrow with it as the horsehair hassocks they knelt on twice on Sundays. 'Yes,' he said again. He was content to let Galbraith tell it.

'It would mean domestic and professional ruin for me if this got out.'

'I think you exaggerate, Phil.' He was sympathetic. 'There aren't many who can boast a strict moral code. No doubt your partners had it off on the side when they were physically capable. There's no virtue in being moralistic when you're too old to be anything else. We're in the swinging, permissive decade now,' he added disapprovingly.

'The legal profession isn't,' Galbraith said. He looked deflated in his flannel suit. 'And you aren't being investigated,' he pointed out. 'I am.'

'Don't fret. I'm not going out of here and give an interview about it on television. But you haven't told me enough about your relationship with her. Was it a commercial one?'

'Oh, Christ, George,' the solicitor protested. 'You make it sound so damned sordid.'

'Well? Was it?'

'I gave her small gifts,' he defended himself. 'She allowed me to help her financially. She received only the hundred a month from her husband. It just wasn't enough ...'

'What do you call a small gift?'

Galbraith shifted in his chair. 'Are you asking me to confirm what you already know?' He was getting prickly.

'Probably. But please answer my question.'

'Ten pounds now and then. Something of that order. It helped.'

'She could have got herself a job.'

'That, George,' he said sharply, 'was her decision. She was frightened, anyway.'

'Oh?'

'She was sure her husband was watching her.'

Rogers lifted his eyebrows. 'You were taking a chance if he was. Most unsolicitorlike.'

'No. She knew when he was on a night-flying schedule.'

'Why was she frightened of him?'

'He used to hit her during their marriage . . . he had a foul temper. He also wanted a divorce pretty badly.'

'Tell me about her, Phil. Unbutton your natural caution just a bit. Even the trivialities might help.' He cocked his head at him. 'And you do want to help me, don't you?'

'Bugger you, George,' he snorted. 'I'm more concerned about my own troubles.'

'Come on, Phil,' Rogers urged. 'Tell me what sort of a woman she was.'

'I'm relying on your friendship, George.'

Rogers, busy cramming tobacco into his pipe, grunted, 'Come off it, Phil. You've known me long enough. We needn't get sentimental about it.'

'Damn you.' Galbraith poured another brandy and lit a cigarette. 'It wasn't anything other than some extramarital entertainment.' He was trying hard to reduce his admissions to the level of clubroom chit-chat. 'I used to telephone her and make an appointment. Whatever the time of year I would arrive after dark, leaving the car in the next road. I'd carry a briefcase to give me some sort of cover.' His lips quirked. 'She treated each visit like an elaborate indoor picnic. We had everything but a bloody Fortnum and Mason's hamper and an aerosol of fly repellant. She'd keep me at arm's length until I was damn near puce in the face.' He laughed, seeking understanding from Rogers. The detective smiled with his teeth. 'Then she'd talk. Lord, how she loved talking.'

'What did she talk about?'

'Herself mainly. I remember she told me of her

illustrious father – he was a brain surgeon. How he'd got the District Nurse with child and how her mother and the woman's family had all mucked in and covered things up.' He laughed mirthlessly. 'A commendable custom that seems to have died out. She spoke often of her husband, Dominis. How terrified she was of him. How he used to get drunk and chase her bollock-naked all over the furniture. Of course, she didn't quite put it like that but you get the general idea.'

'Yes, vividly. You handled her separation, Phil, on the grounds of cruelty. How much of it was true?'

Galbraith moved uneasily, pulling at his bottom lip. 'We have, more or less, to accept what we're told in domestic cases. She had no scar tissue, no bruises. But that doesn't signify, of course. Somehow I believed her.' He lost himself for a moment in recollection. Then he smiled ruefully. 'I oughtn't to tell you this. It doesn't show me in a very good light but it underlines my complete frankness. One evening there was a knock on the door. We lay quiet for a few moments hoping whoever it was would go away. Then it sounded as if the door was being battered down. Nancy put on her dressing robe and went to answer it. I heard a man's voice – I couldn't make out what he was saying – and Nancy was expostulating with him, saying it was late and she was in bed. At first I thought it was Dominis and that was enough for me. I put on my pants and socks, grabbed the rest of my stuff and was through the window into the garden. I dressed behind the bushes and got out quickly through the back way.'

'When was this?'

'Months ago. I can't remember exactly when except it was bloody cold with frost on the grass.' His brow furrowed. 'She told me later it was an old friend of her father's calling unexpectedly. But, you know, the voice had something familiar about it.' He shook his head,

94

anticipating Rogers' question. 'It's no good. I've tried and I still can't place it.'

'Anything more, Phil?'

'Christ! I'm being more than obliging.' There was a tiny spark of resentment there.

'I know. It's so nice of you. Did she mention any other man?'

His forehead wrinkled. 'Yes. One man. She said she'd helped the police over the Clancy-Spiteli murders back in June. This man was concerned in the case, I believe. She didn't say anything other than he worried her.'

Nancy Frail had been Lingard's end of the enquiry and Quint had also been concerned in it. Rogers thought he could make his choice between the two of them. 'But no name?'

'No. It was an isolated casual remark. I didn't want to know about it anyway.'

'Did she ever visit you at your home?'

'My *home*!' Galbraith looked astonished. 'Are you mad?'

'Always at her flat?'

'Yes.'

'No Mr and Mrs Smith at small hotels?'

'Your humour is misplaced,' Galbraith said stiffly.

'I'm sorry. You had a key?'

'No.' He stared at the end of his cigarette. 'As I said, it was a casual affair. Nothing emotional. Certainly not permanent.'

'She had others?'

'Affairs? What makes you ask that?' He was annoyed. 'She was basically a nice, well-bred woman.'

'I wondered. Do you know she called one of her cats Philip?'

'Yes.'

'The other six had names.'

'I imagine they did. What are you getting at?'

'They all had men's names. And three of them are she-cats.' He paused. 'You weren't the only one. Some of the others paid by cheque. So I know.'

Galbraith's face was expressionless. He expended his protest by viciously stubbing out the butt of his cigarette. 'You've a bloody cruel streak in you, George.'

'Yes, I have,' he acknowledged as if Galbraith had said he had black hair. 'It makes me ask awkward questions. Like, where were you on Sunday evening the twelfth of October?'

'That's the evening she died?'

'Yes.'

'What if I say I was home with my wife?'

'I'd check if necessary.'

'Damn you. Haven't you any humanity at all?'

'A bit. Where were you?'

'At home. As I said.' He looked anxious. 'But on my own. My wife went to her mother's place. What times do you need to clear me?'

'Say, up to eleven o'clock.'

His eyes were on the chaotic jumble of folded papers and books scattered on his desk. 'She didn't come home that night. It's not unusual. She sometimes stays. I was on my own. But she telephoned at about ten forty-five. I trust you'll take my word for that?'

'No more than I could before.'

'Are you suggesting I'm lying?' There was no friendliness in his eyes now.

'Don't come the court advocate stuff with me, Phil,' Rogers said sharply. 'You lied when you said your relationship with Frail was a professional one. Of course you'd lie. Particularly if you thought you'd get away with it.'

Galbraith swallowed his anger like a piece of jagged tin.

'I'm not lying now. I was at home all day and all night.'

'All right. Can I have one of your head hairs?'

'In God's name, why?'

'To check against one I already have.'

'One of mine?'

'I don't know. That's what I want to find out.'

'I see.' His lips tightened. 'Where was this other hair found?'

Rogers looked at him quizzically, not answering.

'You can't tell me?'

'No.'

'I'm sorry. There's no obligation on me to go that far. It wouldn't be unreasonable to suppose a few of my head hairs are in the flat. Hell, George,' he protested. 'You can see my point of view, surely.'

'Only if you've something to hide. Have you ever been in her car?'

'No.' He asked uneasily, 'Does Mr Huggett know about this?'

'Yes. If it's any consolation to you, he doesn't believe it.' Rogers smiled. 'He's your friend. Would you prefer to disabuse him yourself?'

'You're a bastard, George. You mean as an alternative to your telling him?'

'Somebody has to, Phil.'

'There's no chance . . .'

'No,' Rogers said warningly. 'Don't ask it.'

'Sorry. Can I ask you a question?'

'Of course.'

'Where did Nancy die?' There was a slight tremor in his voice.

'In someone's bed, I imagine. It left the particular owner of it with a pretty problem of disposal.'

'She didn't die in mine. You've got to believe that.'

'Then you needn't worry, need you.'

'I do. You'll respect my position . . . not see my wife unless you have to.'

'I won't see her unless I'm forced to.' He eyed the stocky Galbraith and grinned, not unsympathetically. 'Don't fret, Phil. So far you don't add up to being a very likely suspect. Not just at this moment.'

When Rogers left, the solicitor's handshake was tepid but he managed a pale smile. 'At the moment, I wish I'd never seen the bloody woman. Or you either, George, for that matter.'

The sun had burnt up the clouds and Rogers opened the car window. A warm breeze smelling of canal water and car exhaust fumes blew sparks and ash from his pipe into the back of the car.

Spye Green Hall, pink-bricked and Georgian, was set in a walled area of pruned greenery. Every tree and shrub stood symmetrical with its neighbour; the turf beneath shaved almost to the roots. Rogers approached it through two stone gate pillars decorated with armorial bearings, the car's tyres crunching on thick, freshly raked gravel.

The massive carved oak door was designed to make callers feel they should have slunk in by the tradesmen's entrance. Rogers lifted the heavy brass knocker on it with a forefinger and let it drop. Then he did it again.

The woman who opened the door was no dried-up, juiceless spinster. She was soft-skinned and as well proportioned as an operatic Valkyrie. Her hair was yellow and cut short in small curls like the petals of a chrysanthemum. Her eyes were bright. If she was *virgo intacta* it was, Rogers admitted to himself, doing her the world of good. He could smell the faintest whiff of gin. That was all there was to support his earlier assessment of her to Coltart.

She smiled at him. She had dimples as well. And her

98

teeth were surprisingly white. 'Chief Inspector Rogers,' she said. 'Do come in.' As she turned away the smile dropped and for a moment she looked worried.

He followed her along the corridor, admiring her well-fleshed body in the apricot jersey dress she wore. He could discern the outline of her briefs beneath it. They were very small briefs.

Her brother was in his study. He sat at a huge desk as if granting a vice-regal audience. He neither rose, offered to shake hands nor asked Rogers to sit.

When his sister had closed the door behind her, he said, 'And what can I do for you, chief inspector?' His manner was such that Rogers wanted to hit him.

He was a big man with smooth, buttery blond hair. His features were blobby and puffed out with his pomposity. He wore a hairy Harris tweed suit, a pheasant-shooter's check shirt and a purple and green college tie.

Rogers noted a current copy of Debrett's *Baronetage, Knightage and Companionage* on his desk. That didn't surprise him. Wallace would be in it. There were also copies of *The Farmer and Stock-Breeder* and *The British Friesian Journal*. An empty coffee cup and a plate of charcoal biscuits were on a silver tray. To the detective, he looked just the man to savour the flimflammery and fake feudalism of a political knighthood.

Rogers waited to be asked to sit. When he wasn't, he said, 'I'm making enquiries into the death of a woman called Nancy Frail. You know of her? And of her death?'

'Yes. It was in the newspapers. Why have you come to me?'

'Miss Frail was found dead in her own car. She appears to have died naturally from a coronary thrombosis. Later, however, she was left in a lane not far from here. The circumstances require my checking on her associates.'

'I still say, why have you come to me?'

99

'I thought you might like to tell me about your own association with her.' Rogers kept him pinned with his eyes, noting his reaction. There wasn't much of one.

'Just what do you mean by that, chief inspector?' He was trying to intimidate the detective; trying to make him feel like one of his herdsmen asking for an undeserved rise in pay. Apart from his natural contempt for titles, he was damned now if he was going to call him 'Sir Andrew'.

'I'm asking you if you had an association with Miss Frail.'

'If I did, I'm not so sure it would be any of your business.'

'If you did, I'm just as sure it would,' Rogers said calmly.

Wallace got up from the desk and stood with his back to the fire. It was burning sawn blocks of wood and smelt like autumn.

'I don't particularly like your attitude, chief inspector.'

'Oh? In what way?' Rogers asked politely. It was a deceptive politeness.

'I'd like you to remember who I am.'

Rogers almost smiled. Had Wallace two chins he would have led with them both. 'I know you are Sir Andrew Wallace and a Justice of the Peace. Is that what you mean?'

Wallace flushed with anger. 'As you choose to put it like that, yes.'

Rogers' manner was dangerously quiet. 'You mean I didn't knuckle my forehead? Call you Sir Andrew every other word?' Being left standing had put a cutting edge to his dislike. 'Are you complaining because I'm not crawling around you like a bloody lap dog?'

There was a quietness of shocked incredulity. Somewhere in another part of the house Rogers could hear the droning of a vacuum cleaner being used.

There were pink blotches on Wallace's cheeks when he spoke. 'How dare you, chief inspector.' He was shaking with anger. 'I meant nothing of the sort. Your attitude is insolent . . . outrageous.'

'And yours is arrogant,' Rogers said harshly. It hadn't taken long for the two men to start fighting and Rogers was taking a calculated risk in what he said. When Wallace started to say something, he interrupted, 'Wait a moment. Are you saying you're immune from being questioned by a police officer? That you expect special privileges? Is that it?' His fierce glare forced an answer from Wallace's pomposity.

'No, I do not. It depends on their form.'

In Rogers' opinion, Wallace had very little above his collar stud and it showed. He was uncertain of what he could do with the blackbrowed, challenging detective.

'Only, if you *do* consider yourself privileged,' Rogers pressed him, 'I'll be quite happy to make my enquiries about your association with Miss Frail elsewhere.'

Wallace puffed his cheeks. 'Is that a threat?'

'Yes.'

Wallace presented his back to Rogers and kicked at the logs in the fire. When he turned he had contained his anger although it still glowed in his eyes. In a choked voice he said, 'Ask your questions, chief inspector.' He didn't say, *and then get out* but Rogers knew that was what he meant. 'I warn you, however, I shall be complaining of your conduct to Huggett.'

'I expect you to,' Rogers said with indifference. 'While you are doing so, remember the terms of my office. They include the phrase, "without fear or favour". I don't recall their mentioning there were certain people they didn't apply to.'

'I repeat, ask your questions,' he ground out.

'Did you know Miss Frail?'

'I did.'

'In what connection?'

'I purchased something from her.'

'A collection of French Louis Napoleon stamps?'

Wallace's eyes jerked his surprise. 'Yes.'

'When?'

'In June of last year.'

'How much did you pay for it?'

'That's my business.'

'And mine. Was it £850? Paid by cheque?'

'You seem to know all about it.'

'Show me the stamps, please.'

He hesitated, then went behind the desk and crouched down before a small green safe. He turned a key in the lock and wrenched at its handle. From its interior he took a slim blue album. He placed it on the desk and opened it carefully. He seemed reluctant to expose it to Rogers' inspection.

The detective examined the stamps hinged to the black pages. They were interleaved with sheets of transparent paper. The fifty or so stamps were unused and in mint condition. The ten-centime bistre Rogers had checked on was there. He indicated it with his finger. 'That one's catalogued at £650. What is the value of the lot?'

There was all the cupidity of possession in the man's eyes. 'In *Thiaude's* catalogue, about £1700. But that,' he hastened to say, 'is a different thing from the market value. I paid Miss Frail the current valuation.'

Rogers was disbelieving. 'Half the catalogue value? Is that normal?'

'Perfectly normal. You obviously know nothing of stamps.'

Rogers closed the album. 'I know these were stolen abroad. Then smuggled through the customs.'

Wallace's jaw dropped. He looked from the stamps to

Rogers and back again. 'What did you say?' he demanded in a strangled voice.

'I said they were stolen. Then smuggled into this country.'

'Rubbish!' His face reddened. 'They were willed to Miss Frail by her father some years ago. He was a well-known collector.'

'She said that?'

'Yes.'

'You don't know it as a fact?'

'No.'

'Why was she selling them?'

'She had very little income.'

'She lied to you,' Rogers said flatly. 'She had a good income and the stamps came from her husband.'

'I don't believe it. Can you prove your outrageous allegations?'

'Her income is a matter of fact. I propose checking through Interpol to find out about the stamps. I'll certainly know when we find Dominis.'

That produced a long silence. 'What do you mean, when you've found Dominis?' Rogers noticed he hadn't asked who Dominis was.

'He's missing.'

'I see.' He turned and kicked at the logs again. 'Then I suggest you spend your time looking for him. Not asking me impertinent questions.' When Rogers remained silent, his face contemptuous, he said, 'What do you propose doing about the stamps?'

'I shall take them as an exhibit. Unless you wish to argue that you can justify the retention of stolen property.'

'Dammit you can't, man.' He was anguished. 'They're unique . . . valuable. The wrong handling . . .'

'I won't hurt them,' Rogers said curtly. 'What do the

words Rajput Cat mean?'

Wallace was furious. 'Have you been snooping around? Prying into my personal affairs before coming here?' His voice shook. 'By God, chief inspector, there'll be an accounting for this.'

'Miss Frail kept a record of such things,' Rogers said calmly. The man was a bladder of wind. 'When she died under the circumstances she did, her affairs naturally became ours.'

Although the voice retained a semblance of confidence, the eyes wobbled. 'She could record nothing about which I need be worried, chief inspector.'

'Good. So what did she mean by Rajput Cat?'

'It was something I gave her. A small painting in tempera colours. Of no great value but she loved cats. Does that satisfy you?'

'What was it like?'

He made rectangular motions in the air with a finger. 'About six inches square. In a black lacquered frame. It showed three female figures and a black cat.'

'Had she hung it?' Rogers couldn't remember seeing the picture.

'I don't know. She intended to.'

'Thank you. Now can I return to the question of your relationship with her. My information is that this year you visited her flat on five occasions and she visited you here on three. Is that correct?'

Wallace's complexion was mottled. 'I see,' he said quietly. He had lost a lot of his pomposity and arrogance. But not enough to make him likeable. 'Why is my social life being subjected to scrutiny by the police? Am I required to account to you for what I do? For what I have done?'

'Not really,' Rogers said mildly. 'But I am fully entitled to ask you questions. You, on the other hand, are entitled to refuse to answer.'

He cleared his throat. 'Miss Frail and I were friends, sharing a common interest in a number of things. There was nothing improper – as you appear to imply – in our relationship.'

'If you say so.' Rogers was non-committal.

'Dammit!' Wallace glared at him. 'I do say. You don't believe me, do you!'

Rogers remained silent on that. He didn't. He said, 'I don't want to waste a lot of time explaining that my only concern with your activities is in any bearing they may have on her death and the disposition of her body. To be blunt, your friendship with her only interests me insofar as that is concerned.' He paused, giving his words full weight. 'And then only if you were the last person to see her alive.'

Wallace said harshly and with emphasis, 'I repeat. I knew her only socially.'

'All right. Then give me some of her social background.'

He considered for a moment then said, 'She was definitely someone you would call a lady. Her interests were cultured and she lived a quiet life with very few friends. She never went out much. I think she wished to avoid her husband from whom she was separated.'

'Did she say why?'

'I believed her fears groundless but she thought he had a gun.'

'And the wish to use it?'

'So she told me.'

'But as a magistrate, you didn't advise her to complain to the police.'

He flushed, plainly resenting the reproof. 'I said I didn't believe the danger existed.'

'H'm.' Rogers showed he wasn't impressed. 'When did you last see her?'

'Last month some time.'

'When were you going to see her again?'

'I had made no arrangements.'

'Miss Frail died on Sunday evening. Would you like to tell me where you were?'

'No, I would not,' he snapped back. He had clearly made up his mind to say no more.

Rogers sighed. He picked up the stamp album. 'You'd like an official receipt for this?'

'Yes. And I know every stamp in it.' His voice trembled. 'God help you, chief inspector, if any harm comes to a single stamp. Or if I find that what you have told me is not true.'

'I'll see myself out,' Rogers said curtly. His spine ached from standing.

Wallace turned his back on him, his face thoughtful now as he stooped to throw a fresh block of wood on the fire.

Rogers didn't see the sister on his way out. He thought she might be busy emptying a gin bottle. Having experienced her brother crowing on his own dungheap, he didn't blame her.

9

The green and white Citroën Safari attracted Rogers' attention mainly because it was parked in a No Waiting area in the town centre. The very downward curve of its bonnet spoke of its arrogance.

Rogers pulled in behind it. There was a snuff-coloured hawk hunched inside on a log perch. It wore a leather hood with red-felt eye patches and a feather plume. A gaunt liver-and-white bitch lay near the bird and growled at Rogers through the window. A parking ticket was stuck to the windscreen.

Rogers lit his pipe and waited.

The little bantam of a man approaching twenty minutes later was easily recognizable. His pointed beard and thin moustache were coppery on a lean brown face that had damn-and-blast-you written all over it. The maroon velveteen jacket he wore with a polo-necked pullover was scruffy but of good cut. The trousers were shapeless and stained. He carried three dead unskinned rabbits under one arm. Two hundred years ago he would have been wearing a big sword and itching to slice somebody's gut with it.

Rogers smiled wryly. It wasn't his day for influencing people or winning friends and there was no reason to suppose it was going to change for the better.

Norton ripped the parking ticket from the windscreen. Without reading it he tore it into confetti and dropped the pieces into the gutter.

'That will still cost you,' Rogers said from behind him.

Norton swung around and glared at the detective. His eyes were slate-grey. 'Who the hell are you, cock?'

Rogers had his warrant card ready in his hand. He showed it to him. 'A few words,' he said, 'about Nancy Frail.'

Norton glanced at the card, unimpressed. 'I'm busy.'

Rogers smiled. 'So am I. But I'll make time to talk to you.' He said it as if doing him a favour. Deliberately.

'Oh, you will, will you?' Norton opened the door of the car. 'You've a bloody nerve, cock. What's it all about?'

Rogers felt happier. He could deal with outright, unconcealed hostility. 'It's about the death of Miss Frail.'

'So I imagined. What's it to do with me?'

'If you'll stop being so aggressive about it, I'll get around to telling you.'

'Tell me.'

'Not in the street. There are people listening and I'm not selling you a set of encyclopaedias.'

Norton showed his teeth between the whiskers. 'Funny bastard, aren't you.' It was a form of approval. He jerked his head. 'Sit in the car, cock. I'll give you five minutes, no more. I'm expecting my wife.' He closed the car door after him, throwing the rabbits in the back.

Rogers smiled again. Norton wasn't too happy about it. He opened the passenger door then paused, wrinkling his nose. The nylon plush seat was dusty and splashed with white.

'What's the matter?' Norton asked. 'You're not shy of a bit of hawkshit, are you?'

Rogers said, 'Yes, I am.'

The little man reached behind him and pulled out a grey blanket. It was covered with dog hairs. He draped it over the seat. 'Fussy bastard! I've had the Lord Lieutenant of the county sit there and he didn't complain.'

As Rogers climbed in the hawk gaped its beak and bated, its striped wings flapping wildly against the canvas screen attached to the perch.

'Also a clumsy bastard,' Norton grunted, reperching the bird. 'She can't stand coppers either.' He leaned back and lit a thin cheroot. 'All right, get cracking.' He was watching Rogers in the rear view mirror.

The detective slid the seat back on its ratchets and stretched his legs. It was comfortable in the big car. He opened a side window. The bitch licked the back of his neck and one cheek. She had bad breath.

'Make yourself at home,' Norton said sarcastically.

'Thank you. Nancy Frail was found dead . . .'

Norton interrupted him. 'Spare me the details, cock, and get down to the nub. I do read the newspapers. I also listen to the radio.'

Rogers continued as if he hadn't spoken. '. . . in her car in a lane near the railway line off Bourne End. Not too far from where you live. She apparently died of a coronary thrombosis. You knew her?'

'You're telling the story.' Norton blew smoke against the glass of the windscreen, thinking hard.

'I understand you saw her on Saturday night. The day before she died.'

'So?'

'So I'd like to know something about it.' Rogers was bland but in no mood to be ambiguous or tactful.

'Why? She wasn't murdered.'

'She was dumped in the lane after she was dead. It's something the Coroner doesn't wholly approve of.'

'Nor me, cock. If I saw her on Saturday as you say, I don't suppose I'd be seeing her Sunday as well.'

'Why not?'

'Oh, Jesus! Don't play cat and mouse with me. You know the score or you wouldn't be sitting so bloody smugly where you are.' He scratched irritably at his small beard with a fingernail. Then he glanced at Rogers cunningly. 'How many ten pounds can a man afford to fling around?'

'Was it worth it?' Rogers was surprised at Norton's frankness after the unpromising start. It was a pleasant change.

'Yes. Or I wouldn't have paid it.'

'Nine times this year?'

Norton shrugged his maroon shoulders. 'If you say so. I never counted.'

'Where were you on Sunday evening?'

He thought for a moment or two. 'Out.'

'Which isn't good enough.'

'And which isn't worrying me, cock, if it isn't.'

'Where?' Rogers insisted.

Norton screwed his eyes against the smoke rising from the cheroot. 'Nosy bastard! First to The Saracen's Head, then The Ironmaster's Arms, then The Minster Hotel. In that order. Does that satisfy you?'

'Not yet. On your own?'

'Yes. I'm a solitary boozer.'

'Who can corroborate all this?'

Norton snorted. 'That's the sort of thing you get paid for. Don't ask me to do your dirty work.'

'All right. It's on your own head.' He held out his hand palm upwards and Norton stared at it. 'Let me have the key she gave you. You won't need it now.'

'Key?' he said blankly.

'The key to her flat.'

'Don't be daft. I never had any key.'

Rogers held the damn-and-blast-you glare for a long time. 'All right. Do you know any other friends of Miss Frail's?'

'God! How you coppers love a smarmy euphemism. You mean paying customers?'

'If you like.'

'She never told me and I didn't ask.'

Rogers took a chance. 'But you knew Harry Quint as one.'

'He told you?'

'He paints birds of prey. He'd know you. You'd know him.'

'For a copper you're a clever bastard.'

'I got it out of a training manual. Did you ever meet her husband?'

'I wouldn't know him if I did. Look,' he said impatiently, 'while I don't give a damn, my wife's due back any minute. She'll only . . .'

'I think she's here,' Rogers said.

Seeing the woman angling towards the Safari, he

remembered her. She was slim with square shoulders and short cropped hair under a floppy hat. She wore an off-white shower coat and buckled red shoes and carried a leather bag with small packages in it. Her features were neat and she looked too good for her husband. Rogers thought sourly that any woman would be too good for him.

He opened his door and got out, holding it open for her. She smiled at him and waited. He noticed her eyes were dark green and her teeth nicely white.

Norton leaned sideways and said, 'I've been clobbered for parking again. Meet the local law.'

'Rogers,' the detective said. 'Your husband's a born loser. It's going to cost him another two pounds.'

She shook his hand. 'It serves him right, Mr Rogers. I've told him so before.'

He shut the door after her. She didn't look the sort of woman to be fooled that easily. To her husband, he said, 'I'll see you around, Mr Norton.'

He beat an approaching traffic warden to his own car by a couple of yards.

After brushing dog hairs from his coat, Rogers entered a telephone kiosk and spoke to Detective Sergeant Hagbourne.

There were two messages left for him. Hagbourne read them out. The first, from Sir Andrew Wallace, asking him to return to Spye Green Hall as soon as possible. The second – from the laboratory – stated that the hair taken from Dominis' cap was identical in its colour, scale formation and in the measurement of its medulla to that found on the deceased woman's clothing.

Both messages pleased him. 'Has the Chief Constable been asking for me?' he asked Hagbourne.

'Yes. Round and about.'

'He left instructions?'

'Only to let him know when you'd returned. I told him you were booked out on general enquiries.'

'Good. You know Waldo Norton the falconer?'

Hagbourne laughed. 'I knocked his gin and vermouth over once. He wanted me to go outside and fight. I had a bit of a job to get out from under. I know him all right.'

Rogers knew Norton had been lucky that Hagbourne had refused his challenge. The sergeant could macerate an opponent into a bloody pulp with his small bony fists.

'Do a check on him. He's supposed to have visited The Saracen's Head, The Ironmaster's Arms and The Minster on Sunday evening. If he did, someone saw him. I'm on the way to Spye Green Hall if you want me.'

Wallace answered the door to Rogers. He was in no better mood and motioned him curtly to enter. But he surprised him in the study by asking him to sit.

Wallace remained standing. 'Chief inspector,' he said, still the *grand seigneur*, 'distasteful as this matter has been, I have spoken to my sister about it. In order that you should make no unpleasant and possibly damaging enquiries about my movements, she would be prepared to corroborate that I spent the Sunday evening here at home.'

'Which is what you did?'

'Of course.' Wallace gestured his irritation. 'Dammit, I find it difficult to stomach your continued scepticism.'

Rogers was urbane. 'I don't disbelieve you. Why should I? If your sister will corroborate it, that's all I require. Your actual association with Miss Frail then ceases to interest me.'

Wallace frowned. 'You mean you want her to tell you herself?'

'It's the form,' Rogers said mildly. 'You can't expect otherwise.'

'I did. But if you insist, she will. Before you do, however, I require your assurance you will treat my affairs with discretion.'

'Naturally.'

Wallace hesitated. 'One thing more. Is it possible for me to obtain the return of my painting?'

'Not through me. You gave it to her and it forms part of her estate.'

'I see.' He looked uncomfortable. 'That is another matter in which I require your discretion. My sister may not understand the reason prompting my giving it . . .'

'I shan't mention it,' Rogers said curtly. 'I'm never very forthcoming. I just like other people to be.' He kept his face wooden. 'Did you have a key to Miss Frail's flat?'

A spasm of anger twisted Wallace's mouth. 'Damn you, *no*! You've a marked aptitude, chief inspector, for being too blunt.'

'It's only a question,' Rogers said with an irritatingly amiable smile, 'and you've answered it.'

Wallace moved to the door. 'I'll fetch my sister.'

Rogers said, 'Just a moment, please. I'd like to interview her alone.'

'Oh?' Wallace stopped dead. 'Why?'

'I never interview anybody in the presence of the person we are discussing.'

Wallace drew a deep breath. 'I still propose complaining to Huggett about your manner, chief inspector. I advise you not to make it worse.'

'On her own, please.'

He tried to stare the detective down and failed. He was savage with frustrated anger. Rogers followed him along the corridor. They stopped outside a white door and Wallace tapped on it with the knuckle of his finger.

Constance Wallace opened the door. She showed Rogers her dimples again. Her hair was slightly disordered and the perfume of gin was stronger.

'Mr Rogers wishes to speak to you on your own, Constance,' Wallace said disapprovingly. He was as magisterial with his sister as he had been with Rogers. He turned on his heel and left them.

She smiled at the detective again. 'Please come in, Mr Rogers. I was expecting you.' Her voice was beautifully modulated and meant for opening church bazaars.

The room and its contents appeared to have been handed down by a couple of generations of looters of *objets d'art* from Victorian India. There were lacquered tables in black and scarlet and ebony elephants; brass vases and oriental paintings and sepia-coloured photographs of topeed and heavily moustached polo players; Indian Army officers in self-conscious groups with speared hogs and turbaned retainers holding horses. The room was a monument to a long-dead British Raj. Only the bowls of white flowers in it gave the room femininity. The air was sweet with their scent.

The chairs – probably taken from an officers' mess, Rogers thought – were comfortable and he sat in one.

She went straight to a sideboard and clinked glassware. 'A drink, Mr Rogers?' she asked over her shoulder.

'A gin and tonic, please, if you don't tell anyone,' he replied with a friendly solemnity. Although she had the demeanour of a memsahib in the making about her, he liked what he saw.

They sat companionably, facing each other. She combed her hair back with her fingers. Where the dusty sunshine touched it, it glinted gold. She either had water in her gin or was drinking it straight. He couldn't tell. But she had had more than was usual by midday.

'I have had no experience of being interrogated by a policeman,' she smiled. 'Do you ask me questions?' She took a sip of her gin and put the glass down carefully.

'Yes,' he said. He had placed his own drink untasted on

a coffee table. He would wait to see how the interview progressed. 'Your brother knew a Miss Frail through buying stamps from her. She died on Sunday evening of a coronary thrombosis in circumstances which require I check on everybody knowing her.'

'The thrombosis was a natural one?'

'So far as a post-mortem examination can tell us, yes.'

She nodded. 'I see. I understand there is something wrong with the stamps, that they are stolen property.'

'Yes.' He smiled amiably. It was an expression that sat uneasily on his hawkish face. 'Something your brother need not have known, of course. But I'm more interested in your confirming his whereabouts on Sunday evening, Miss Wallace.' Looking at her, he thought she had the smoothest flesh he had seen on a woman.

'We don't live in each other's pockets, Mr Rogers. He has his study.' She glanced around her. 'I have my room. But if he went out I would know. I would hear his car. Which I didn't.'

'You were here all evening?'

The point of her tongue licked her lips. 'I lead a very quiet life. I don't very often go out.' She occasionally slurred a consonant but it could have been the remains of a lisp.

'But you know he was here?'

'I know he was here.'

'Had you met Miss Frail?'

'No, never,' she said crisply, 'although I knew of her. And knew her by sight. I understand she wasn't quite . . . you understand?'

'I understand.' He considered it safe to drink his gin and tonic.

She regarded him levelly. Her eyes were the amber of warm syrup. 'Just what is the background to a coronary thrombosis that sends a detective chief inspector out investigating it, Mr Rogers? I thought you were reserved for serious crimes.'

'She was dressed and taken to a lane and left there. It isn't something you can do and not invite investigation.'

'What do you mean by being dressed?'

'I believe she was undressed when she died.'

'I see,' she said thoughtfully. 'But nothing nasty . . . seriously criminal?'

'Not that I know of.' Which was less than the truth. But necessary.

She shivered. 'A sordid happening and I don't want to know anything more of it.' She stood and went to the side-board. 'Another drink?'

'Thank you, no.' He held his glass up. 'You've left me behind.'

While she poured another gin, he studied her. He was in a state of relaxed euphoria. He didn't get it very often. When he did he felt free of physical imperfections and mental grittiness; floating a foot above the ground. So he imagined the state of nirvana to be. He liked her as much as he disliked her brother. She was a big woman and moved easily. She wasn't built for the frustrations and boredoms of a spinster's life. He wished he could do some-thing about it. He judged her a strong woman, probably stronger in character than her self-important, strutting brother. Despite the gin. When she sat again her thighs were carelessly exposed. Rogers found it an effort not to look at them. He said, 'I see you're very interested in India.'

'I was.' She seemed in the mood for a talk. Rogers knew what it was to be used as a surrogate priest. She nodded at an open desk, directing his attention to it. He saw a flat portable typewriter and a pile of quarto typescript. 'I've been nearly ten years researching and writing the biography of my grandfather.'

'General Wallace?'

'Yes.' Something in his expression must have prompted her to ask, 'Don't you approve of ancestor worship, Mr Rogers?'

'No. Perhaps because I have none that deserve worshipping.'

'None of mine has done me any good.' She looked wryly in the gin glass. 'I don't suppose you give a damn for the British Raj either?'

'Not really,' he admitted cautiously.

'I can't think many people do. It was a different world. People now . . . they have different standards . . . are less inclined to be moral.' She was introspective.

'Are they?' Rogers twitched his mouth. *She knows*, he told himself. *The pompous sod hasn't got away with a thing.* He said, 'I think the Victorians and Edwardians were just as immoral. Only they didn't make a song and dance about it. They hid the dirt under antimacassars and behind lace curtains.' He nearly said under their bustles but thought better of it. 'Immorality's only condemned by social convention anyway. It depends what you mean by morality.'

'Being a policeman, I suppose you must possess all the virtues?' If there was any irony in her voice, he couldn't detect it.

'Good God, no,' he said, astonished. 'Did I sound all that bluenosed? I suppose we have our smutty little secrets like everyone else. Even the Queen's Police Medal is no guarantee of morality.' His swarthy face was discomposed. 'You embarrass me.'

She laughed delightedly. 'I can talk to you. Do you mind? You don't want to dash off somewhere?'

'I'm flattered. Perhaps I can have that second gin you offered me.'

While she got it for him, he said, 'You are proud of your grandfather, Miss Wallace?'

There was a large photographic portrait of him on the wall. He sported mutton-chop whiskers and a bushy beard. The left side of his tunic was running out of space for medal ribbons. He looked the sort of man who had flogged punkah-wallahs for exercise and the glory of the British Empire.

She had refilled her own glass as well. 'I've written about three hundred thousand words extolling his undoubted virtues,' she said owlishly. She giggled, not happily. 'Then I discovered my hero was an old lecher. That he made regular contributions to the population of Anglo-Indian hybrids.'

'You were surprised?' Rogers knew she wasn't talking only of her grandfather. She was drawing a not very subtle parallel with her brother. 'It was probably the in-thing in India at that time.'

'I was shaken.'

'You shouldn't be. You were putting him on an impossibly high pedestal.'

'But he was the best kind of Englishman, Mr Rogers.'

'You could say Julius Caesar was the best kind of Roman. But the fact remains his sexual habits don't bear too much scrutiny.'

'Julius Caesar wasn't my grandfather, Mr Rogers.'

They both laughed.

'You make too much of it,' he said positively. He waved a hand around the room. 'Your grandfather collected all this?'

'Most of it.'

'And the paintings?'

The gin in the glass she held in her hand didn't slop over. Not quite. 'Those too,' she said slowly, her expression non-committal, shutting him out. 'You are interested in them?'

'They're unusual. What are they?'

'What is generally called Rajput art. Rajputa paintings are usually religious in theme although those are not. They aren't particularly valuable but I think a lot of them.'

'I like them,' he lied. They were too garish for his taste. If there had ever been one showing a cat with three women it wasn't there now.

He squinted at his empty gin glass. 'You make these strong.' He felt he had known her always.

She took it and refilled it. She was friendly again now they weren't discussing Rajput paintings. 'I suppose you think I drink too much?' she said calmly. For the second time she had succeeded in astonishing him.

'It's *your* medicine,' he observed. 'As it is sometimes mine.'

'Not a medicine. A panacea for a wasted ten years of research on the British Army in Rawalpindi and Peshawar. And three hundred thousand words of uncritical gush.'

'But you aren't disillusioned enough to chuck it all up?'

'Oh, yes I am. I only hope I can adjust.' She looked at him oddly. 'And I do want to adjust, Mr Rogers. To a lot of things.'

There was a knock at the door and it opened. Wallace put his head round it. 'Have you finished, Constance?' he asked reprovingly. 'It's nearly time for luncheon.'

She was short with him. 'I won't keep you waiting, Andrew.'

When he had gone she stood, not swaying but definitely holding herself steady. She said, 'Will you come again? I enjoyed our conversation.'

'I'd like to. But I think, somehow, your brother doesn't approve of me.'

'*I* am asking you, Mr Rogers,' she said, her hand warm and soft in his.

He felt an immense friendliness for her and it showed, he supposed. 'I will,' he promised her and meant it. He hoped the sun wasn't going to be bright outside. It wouldn't do his pre-lunch gins any good.

It didn't and he screwed his eyes against it. As he passed Wallace's Daimler in the drive, he stopped and looked at it. It had a rack fitted to the interior to hold two shotguns. It also had two cigar lighters and a pull-out picnic tray with a compartment for bottles of champagne. There were nine enamelled club badges – most of them French – on a bar over the front bumper telling the world what an important man the owner knew he was.

It was then that the thought hit him that Constance Wallace, despite her use of gin as a crutch, was a very clever woman.

10

The Henri et Camille bistro sold the only coffee in town that Rogers didn't consider tepid slop, tasting of old dish cloths. The menu outside said *Spécialités Particulières Couscous et Coq au Vin*. Rogers never ordered anything there more exotic than a sandwich.

With a Gallic sense of the fitness of things, the kitchen was clinically clean, the toilets uncared for; on the basis, Rogers assumed, that one didn't eat or drink in the latter.

Fat Henri was proud of his butter-cooked food and his wife. He told everybody unable to avoid listening that in his forty-odd years of marriage, he had never looked at another woman. Which seemed an absurd improbability. Particularly as Madame possessed, apart from a surly disposition, a pronounced squint in one dark snapping eye and a silky black moustache under a hooked nose.

'*Ah, Monsieur le Flic,*' he greeted Rogers amiably. 'The *Préfecture* is searching for you. Sergeant 'Agbourne wishes to speak to you in 'aste.'

'Coffee and sandwiches first,' Rogers said. 'Whatever it is will keep until I've finished.' What he wasn't cognizant of couldn't interfere with his eating. He suspected Huggett was on his tail and chasing him to earth.

While he watched Henri making his sandwiches with soft French bread and slices of glistening pink ham, he thought of Bridget. They were, in retrospect, pleasant thoughts. His conscience was on the mend.

He ate leisurely from a small formica-covered table, writing up notes of his interviews. He thought wryly that it would help if he could recognize what or who he was looking for. He was a blind man poking his stick ahead of his toes into impenetrable darkness.

When he had finished, he went to the counter and used the telephone. He dialled the Headquarters number and asked for Sergeant Hagbourne.

Hagbourne said, 'I've called every bar and coffee house in town for you. I was about to start on the churches. We've found the car.'

'Agh!' Rogers was happy again. 'Dominis's?'

'What's left of it. It's been dumped at the back of The Glue Pot and looks as if somebody's had his throat cut in it.'

The lane at the rear of The Glue Pot café was squalid and rubbish strewn. The base of its whitewashed wall was stained coffee-coloured with the urine of a thousand customers from the café. To leave a car like a Sunbeam Stiletto there was the act of a madman, providing an irresistible carcass for thieves to pick at. And those living near or frequenting The Glue Pot were nearly all thieves.

The car stood against the wall like a shattered black

beetle, its wheels missing, its axles propped on four piles of housebricks. Children with depraved adult minds had chalked and scratched lavatorial indecencies on its shiny flanks. The number plates had been levered off; the lamp reflectors and bulbs, the wing mirrors, had all been stolen. The window glass had been smashed and the radio and instrument gauges ripped out, leaving nothing but coloured wires behind. Had it been left undiscovered for another night, the engine would have been unbolted and taken and the inside completely gutted. Then the useless shell would have rotted and rusted in the uncaring grey lane until an official of the Corporation Salvage Department tripped over it and caused it to be hauled away.

'They left the ashtray,' Rogers observed to Hagbourne as he regarded the dismembered Sunbeam. 'Which was goddam considerate of them.'

But he wasn't concerned with the cannibalistic dismantling of the car. His interest was canalized in the black gouts of blood he saw on the rubber floor matting and on the smeared foulness on the leather covering of the passenger seat; in the scraping of crushed stone on the control pedals and matting of the driver's side. In the stone powder he saw tiny flakes of yellow and ash-grey. Magnified under his pocket lens they appeared to be fragments of moss or lichen.

Covering the controls with a sheet of polythene and being careful not to touch the steering wheel, he fitted himself comfortably and easily into the driving seat.

When he and Hagbourne had finished their examination, he had the car's remains hoisted into a flat-bed lorry and taken to the police garage.

The two scientific officers he had summoned from the laboratory were already there. 'I want you,' Rogers said, 'to first of all confirm the blood. Then to identify the stone dust for me. You might also look particularly for a

122

contact lens somewhere in the car.' He looked at his watch. It was nearly three. 'How long?' he asked.

Dagg, the biologist, said, 'Don't you ever want anything tomorrow?' He was an old friend of Rogers and could be allowed some sarcasm.

'No.'

'You want us to ignore the demands of the other seven forces in the region? To give you preferential treatment?'

Rogers smiled. 'Of course.'

'Somehow we thought you would,' Dagg observed drily. 'Is an hour or two's working like one-armed paperhangers and ignoring scientifically accepted testing procedures any good?'

'Thanks, John. I need the information today.'

Dagg snorted. 'You surprise me.'

When Rogers knocked at Huggett's office door the effects of the gin had worn off, taking his euphoria with them. He felt stale and stiff-jointed. He thought it would be nice to sit in a hot bath and read a book without worrying. To be able to smoke his pipe in the tranquillity of an overstuffed armchair. The trouble with a murder enquiry was that it wouldn't stand still waiting for the investigating officer to catch up with it. It meant eating sandwiches and wearing dirty shirts and living with the grinning monkey of possible failure on one's back.

Huggett was peppery and pacing his green Wilton with short irritable steps. Each time he reached his sleeping spaniel he would step over or around her as if she were a natural immovable obstacle.

'A most embarrassing day,' he trumpeted at Rogers as he entered the office. 'I've had Galbraith telling me about his liaison with that dreadful woman. I don't know who was the more distressed.' He wagged his head disbelievingly, incredulously. 'How can I ever ask the man to my

123

home again,' he challenged Rogers as if it were his fault.

The detective waited, his expression saturnine, allowing the wash of words to flow over him.

'Then Sir Andrew.' Huggett's eyes blinked. 'I expected, I demanded, some discretion and tact from you. Not this witch-hunting, this stripping a man of the decencies . . .' He put on his colonel-of-the-regiment look. 'He complains you were insolent, that you used the word "bloody" in most offensive terms.'

'Sir Andrew Wallace – with respect – could do with a lesson or two in courtesy himself.' Rogers was coldly annoyed. 'To support that political handout of a title he's got. Nothing short of my kissing his ass would have suited him.'

'There is no need for vulgarity, Mr Rogers,' Huggett said frostily.

'He makes me want to be vulgar,' Rogers snapped. 'And he needs reminding at frequent intervals that we aren't his servants. He's a pompous bore and too full of his own imagined importance.'

'He *is* a magistrate and not lightly to be offended. Certainly not on a minor matter such as this. I warned you . . .'

'So you did.' Roger stuck his underjaw out aggressively. 'And I asked if you were prepared to instruct me to discontinue the enquiry. Which you weren't.' His anger was frothing up. He had always been intolerant of rebuke. 'Despite Wallace's complaint – which I think is a bluff anyway – I'm satisfied I dealt with him properly. He's a liar and in exactly the same league as Galbraith. But without his guts.'

Huggett slapped his flat hand on the desk in an excess of spleen, sliding a filing tray of papers across its shiny surface to fall on the floor. 'If you were investigating a serious crime I could understand it!' he yelled, his complexion mottled crimson. The spaniel flinched and growled at Rogers. It seemed to have more than its natural share of sycophancy.

'It so happens I am,' Rogers said brusquely.

'No you are not. You're investigating trivialities best buried and forgotten. A tuppeny-ha'penny death from natural causes and the unproved theft of some postage stamps. It's not a sufficient justification for you to go barging in with both feet . . . causing God-knows-what trouble in doing it.'

'I'm investigating a murder now,' Rogers said flatly. 'So that takes care of the trivialities.'

Huggett stopped pacing and stared at the flinty face of his subordinate. 'You're *sure*?'

Rogers bristled. 'Of course I'm sure.'

'Good God!' He went to his desk and dropped back into his swivel chair. 'Why the devil didn't you say?'

'Because you never gave me the chance. We've been discussing Wallace and Galbraith.'

'Shut up, blast you!' Huggett snarled at the bitch who was still growling at Rogers. He would have liked to have said it to the detective. 'Tell me now.'

Rogers detailed the finding of Dominis's car and what he had seen in it. 'The blood didn't come from a nose-bleed,' he said. 'It's thick, dead man's blood from the belly. The only conclusion possible is that somebody got himself killed. Either Quint or Dominis. As an outside chance, some X component we know nothing about.'

Huggett threw in his hand. He reached for the telephone. 'I'd better let Sir Andrew know. Cool him off a bit.'

Rogers reacted sharply. 'No, sir. That won't do any good at all. Let him sweat blood for a bit. I may get some more information from him.'

Huggett hesitated, then shrugged. 'As you wish. But

you'll have to justify what you've told me.'

'So I will.'

'What are you going to do now?'

'Look for a body. It shouldn't be too difficult,' he said rashly. He had recovered some of his good humour. 'Something about six feet long, eighteen inches wide and beginning to smell a bit. It couldn't have been all that easy to dispose of.'

Hagbourne was waiting for him outside Huggett's office. A thin man with a pessimistic moustache and pouched brown eyes, he possessed a brash sense of humour.

'I couldn't help overhearing the uproar,' he said. 'Have you been reduced to the ranks?'

'Damn near,' Rogers growled. 'But don't go buying champagne on the strength of it. What's the trouble now?'

'Coltart. He's at Midgley's and asking for you to go there urgently. He wouldn't say why on the telephone.'

'I'm on the way. You go to Spaniards Rise and check on Quint's return. If he's there, grab him and hang on.'

Hagbourne said, 'Don't you want to know about Waldo Norton?'

'Not too anxiously.'

'Well, you're going to now I've done the checking. He was seen in The Saracen's Head and The Ironmaster's Arms but not in The Minster. The last sighting of him was at about nine o'clock in the Ironmaster's. He was then three parts cut.'

Rogers considered for a second or so. 'I'm not very interested in him now,' he said. 'Don't take it any further for the time being.'

Coltart answered the door to his ringing, coming out and closing it behind him. 'Before you go in,' he rumbled, jerking a banana-sized thumb over his shoulder. 'Lingard's been here pumping Midgley.'

'What!' Rogers stared at him, his jaw muscles bunched. 'When was this?'

'Last night.'

'The bloody fool!' he rasped. 'Now he has done it.'

Coltart held a blue plastic frame in one big fist.

'You've done the Photo-fit?' His mind was still on Lingard.

The sergeant offered it to him. 'The best Midgley could do with that bitch of a woman nagging in his ear.' He laughed deep in his belly. 'It's Salvador Dali in a blond wig although I can't imagine him being involved.'

Rogers examined it critically, holding it at arm's length. 'Quint wouldn't be flattered but it could certainly be a worm's-eye view of him.' He gave it back to Coltart. 'I'll speak to Midgley,' he said sombrely, 'and God help Lingard if he's interfering.'

'Then God help him,' Coltart muttered under his breath, 'because the sod is.'

The fat woman was still a flaccid hulk of pink flesh on the blue satin settee. She looked at Rogers as if he were a court bailiff repossessing unpaid-for furniture from a crippled widow. By her side was a loaded three-tier cake stand. She was pouring tea into her robin's-bum of a mouth from a tiny gilt and scarlet cup.

Midgley sat unhappily in a chair, a fuming cigarette held between the fingers of a limp hand. 'I should be back in my office, Mr Rogers,' he began querulously, eyeing his wife, indicating who had initiated his complaint.

'Ten minutes only,' Rogers promised briskly. 'So tell me about Mr Lingard's visit.'

Midgley flapped a hand in the direction of Coltart. 'As I told the sergeant, he called here last night. At eight-fifty exactly.' His Adam's apple bobbed. 'He said he wanted to recheck the statement I had made. In case I'd forgotten something vital.'

'So you went all through it again? Told him everything?'

'Yes. I'm sorry . . .'

The woman's expression was a fat belittling contempt. She said, 'H'm' through a mouthful of meringue.

Rogers scowled at her on behalf of her unwilling husband. 'You weren't to know,' he assured him, although he cursed him silently. 'Sergeant Coltart has now told you Mr Lingard isn't on the case?'

'Yes. But last night, I naturally thought . . . his being a detective, you understand?'

'Don't worry about it. What was his attitude?'

'Attitude? Oh, yes. Correct enough, I suppose, in what he actually said. But not very polite. I mean, he didn't say thank you or please.' He hesitated. 'He was very angry about something. He wouldn't sit down.' He glanced at his wife and moistened his lips with a yellow-furred tongue.

'Tell them,' she hissed at him.

'Er . . . yes. He smelled of alcohol. And his manner was most odd. He kept taking snuff and mumbling to himself. I thought . . .' He trailed off apologetically.

'You thought what?' Rogers pushed him.

'I thought he was a little unbalanced . . . you know?'

'But you told him just the same.'

'I knew he was a policeman. I could hardly not.'

'Tell them about his car,' the woman's spiteful voice ordered.

Midgley shuttered his eyes, looking down at his hands clasped on his lap. 'I'm sorry. I remembered after you'd gone that I'd seen Mr Lingard's Bentley go past on Sunday evening. No more than that.'

Rogers lowered his eyebrows. 'That seems an odd thing

to forget, Mr Midgley,' he said forbiddingly. 'We were discussing him then. And his car.'

Midgley wrung his hands. 'You know . . . another policeman. It never struck me . . .'

The detective made a noise in his throat.

'. . . I'm a peace-loving man. I don't really want to be involved.'

'Well, you are,' Rogers assured him. For a brief moment he was on the woman's side. 'What time did you see his car?'

'About twenty minutes after the Rolls-Royce left.'

'You saw the driver?' Rogers thought, *The little sod spends all his spare time poking his nose out of the window.*

'Only momentarily but it was Mr Lingard. And he was on his own. He didn't stop, just slowed down and looked at Miss Frail's windows. I suppose he saw there were no lights showing and went on.'

Rogers cocked his head. 'And weren't there?'

Midgley's bald head flushed red. 'I . . . I assumed not,' he faltered. 'Having seen her leave in the Rolls.'

'I thought we'd agreed that was not proven?'

The little man shrugged helplessly. 'I don't know.' His wife visibly sneered at what she had married.

'But you're sure it was Mr Lingard's Bentley?'

'Yes, I'm sure.'

The woman spoke. 'She was a whore.' She said it as if stating a fact nobody else had the wit to recognize.

Rogers regarded her impassively, giving nothing away. 'What makes you say that?'

'You're fools if you think otherwise.' She bit the words out, nodding in the direction of her wilting husband. 'She'd have had him too if I hadn't been around.'

Midgley's head again flushed red and he opened his mouth, gobbling soundlessly like a fish.

'She was rotten. Filthy rotten and diseased.' The tiny mouth spat crumbs of cake on to the carpet.

'Thelma,' Midgley managed to get out. 'You mustn't slander . . . she's dead . . .'

She ignored him. 'I used to hear them at it.' Her currant eyes were prurient. 'Disgusting animals.'

'I'm sure they were if you say so,' Rogers said, tongue in cheek. 'Do you know any of them?' The woman's malevolence fascinated him.

'No, I don't,' she snapped, looking hard at her husband. 'And if I did I wouldn't tell you.'

Midgley was half-way through his third tortured and crumpled cigarette when Rogers and Coltart left. The fat woman was watching her husband with baleful eyes creased by the eating of a jam sponge slice. It made the little man's wish to be back at his office very understandable.

Before leaving the building, Rogers unlocked the door to Nancy Frail's flat and the two men searched it again. Nowhere was there a painting of a cat with three female figures. Nothing but an unoccupied brass hook in a wall that might once have supported it.

11

On his desk, Rogers found a bundle of message forms waiting his attention. Before he read them, he put out two departmental instructions marked Category A Urgency. One required a special search of unoccupied buildings and sheds, parks and gardens, streams and ponds and waste plots for a body. Whose body Rogers couldn't particularize. The other, ordering enquiries to be made to locate Lingard.

He read the message forms. Chief Inspector Godson from Blakehill had called. Dominis had not reported for his pre-flight briefing. Reading between the lines, Rogers got the impression that the C-GA hierarchy were putting pressure on an uncomfortable Chief Inspector Godson to find out why.

Mrs Jane Norton wanted Rogers to telephone her urgently and Dr Dagg of the laboratory had information for him if he could spare some of his valuable time in calling. A note from Hagbourne said that Quint had either not returned or had and gone out again.

There was nothing from Bridget. He lifted the telephone receiver and put a tentative finger on the dial. Then he changed his mind and dialled the Norton number instead. He experienced a tiny warm glow at his act of self-denial. Jane Norton answered as if she had been waiting by the telephone for his call.

'Could you see me, Mr Rogers? I'd like to speak to you.' She hesitated. 'On a confidential matter.'

'Of course. In my office?'

'Here if you wouldn't mind. My husband has the car.'

'I have a call to make first. In half-an-hour?'

Again she hesitated. 'Not any later,' she said. 'I wish to speak to you alone.'

That meant specifically without her husband being around to listen.

Before he left the office, a call came in from the Traffic Department. Lingard's Bentley had been located outside his flat, the engine cold. There was no sign of Lingard and no answer to the repeated ringing of his flat bell.

Rogers found a white-overalled Dagg in the dust-proof, sound-proof examination room of the laboratory.

'Bill's just finished your blood test,' he said. 'He did an old-fashioned microscopical on it. It's either blood from a human being or from an orang-outang. *Homo sapiens* or

Simia satyrus, take your choice. If you're happy you haven't got an orang-outang mixed up in it, he'll plump for its being human. The precipitin test and grouping will have to wait until tomorrow.' He grinned at Rogers. 'He's guessing madly but says it's probably from the stomach.'

'Did he say why?'

'It's slightly turbid for a start and there's so much of it. Then there's marked clotting. But it *is* only inspired guessing. You can't have it all ways.'

'Can he put a date to it?'

'Fairly fresh. But anything less than three days is fresh to Bill.'

'And the dust?'

'Ah, my province. Although I used the petrographic microscope, I'm guessing too. But provisionally, common or garden carboniferous limestone with a *soupçon* of volcanic rock in it.'

'And what does that tell us?'

'That it's come from the moors. It's there in the form of outcrops. I think on the last count by the Ordnance Survey people there was about two thousand acres of it. All good rough going.'

'Clever stuff. I don't know what I'd do without you,' Rogers growled ungraciously.

'Fail lamentably, my friend.' Dagg handed him a glass microscope slide. In its hollow centre was a fragment of dark grey material. 'That's *Cladonia coccifera*. A lichen which grows on exposed limestone. I put them both together and came up with what I consider to be a scientifically inspired conclusion.'

'That the driver of the car has been hiking around on the moors?' Rogers took a gloomy view of that. There was so much of it and all in the open air. Most of the time in very water-logged air. 'I don't suppose you can say he walked with a limp and had a seafaring uncle, Sherlock?'

'No. But give me time,' Dagg said cheerfully. 'I might be able to tell you whether the lichen grows on the north side or the south of the outcrop.'

Rogers thought about that all the way to Goshawk House. He hadn't been there before. It was a timbered, thatched-roofed cottage with an unkempt yew tree covering too many of its small windows.

A row of wire-netting compounds filled one wall of the large enclosed garden. In one was an eagle with a disgruntled expression, tethered to a stump of wood. In the others were perched falcons, hawks and owls. The sun was throwing long shadows and the birds were fluffing their feathers against the growing chill. Shreds of rabbit fur and clean-picked bones littered the compounds. In several there were the broken bodies of tiny yellow chicks. Rogers disliked Norton for that alone.

Jane Norton answered his knocking, neat in a blue velvet dress.

'Waldo's flying a falcon at High Moor,' she said. 'He won't be back for some time.'

The room into which she led him was low-ceilinged and oak-beamed, suitable for an old lady and the sewing together of interminable patchwork bedspreads. Jane Norton was anything but.

Rogers saw her as an attractive woman with a ballet dancer's lithe, small-breasted body. Looking at her he experienced a nagging familiarity. Her face was finely drawn and taut with a sad mouth In five years she could be gaunt, her face lined. But now she was very attractive and desirable. Despite the dark shadow of worry in her eyes.

She sat him on a settee and took a chair opposite. She tucked her dress primly under her thighs.

'I appreciate your work is confidential,' she began, 'but when it concerns interviewing my husband I think I should know.' She was a very direct woman. 'That non-sense about the parking this morning . . .'

Rogers measured her cautiously. 'It was nonsense, of course. But not of my making. On the other hand, the truth is nothing very important.'

'What was it about?' she asked. There was an obstinate resolve in her manner that put him on his guard.

'I was asking his help in a small enquiry,' he said evasively.

'Please be honest with me. Was it about Nancy Frail?'

'You know her?'

'You dodge the issue like a politician, Mr Rogers. Was it?'

He shifted uneasily on the settee. 'I could tell you it's none of your business, Mrs Norton. That you should ask your husband.'

'I have,' she said calmly. 'That's why I asked you to come here.'

'He told you?'

'Of course he didn't.'

He cursed Norton in his mind. Then he temporized with ambiguities. 'It's true I'm enquiring into the death of Miss Frail. And when I'm investigating a case, I ask all sorts of questions of all sorts of people.' He smiled reassuringly. 'Bishops, solicitors, jockeys, window cleaners, falconers . . . the lot. It means nothing.'

'Tell me why you think Waldo should know anything about her death.'

'He could know *of* her.'

'He could be one of her lovers, you mean.'

When he looked at her politely, not answering, she said, 'Please, Mr Rogers. Is he in trouble?'

'You shouldn't jump to conclusions.' *Christ*, he said to himself, *save me from determined women*. 'I repeat. It's a formal enquiry and there's no suggestion he's involved in anything. Miss Frail died a natural death. She died, in fact, from a heart condition. But she was taken to a lane and left there. Which makes it my business.'

'So I understand.'

'Good. Then there's no problem,' Rogers said lightly.

'Your diplomacy isn't very accomplished.' She was not unfriendly. 'I know about Waldo and Miss Frail, Mr Rogers, so you needn't beat so wildly about that particular bush. I just want your assurance he isn't in any trouble.'

'You're worried about him?'

Her sad mouth tightened. 'I don't wish to become the subject of public gossip. Would you like to be cuckolded and the town know of it?'

'That's different,' Rogers said weakly, caught off balance. She was very direct. 'In any case nobody's talking about that.'

'Nonsense,' she said crisply. 'You haven't given me one straight answer.'

Rogers felt a surge of baffled resentment and stood. His face was dark with irritation. 'I'm not a public information bureau, Mrs Norton,' he growled. 'You're not going to use me to flog a confession or something out of your husband.'

'Please sit down, Mr Rogers,' she asked him. 'I'm sorry to have been so blunt. You've told me most of what I wanted to know anyway.' She paused, eyeing him. 'I used to know Nancy Frail.'

He regarded her steadily for several moments, then sat. 'What do you know about her?'

'Are you going to be so tight-lipped about what I tell you as you are about Waldo?' A faint smile lightened her mouth.

'I wouldn't be surprised.' He was attracted to this woman. There was a quite tangible *rapport* between them even in their minor skirmishing. He could like her and not equate her with a bed. Which was unusual for Rogers.

'She is actually married. To a man called Park Dominis. You know?'

'Yes.'

'You know she divorced her first husband?' Seeing the look in his eyes, she said, 'I see you don't. He was an American, an assistant military attaché or similar at the Embassy. I was never quite sure but he carried a CD plate on his car. He returned to America about five years ago. Immediately after the divorce.'

'She told you his name?'

'I met him a few times. Swerdloff. Eugene Swerdloff. With two "f"'s.'

'How long were they married?'

'A year. No more.'

'A woman of many parts,' Rogers murmured. 'He divorced her?'

'No, she him.' She looked at a point over his shoulder, unwilling to meet his gaze. 'I believe the reason was their disagreement over his unpleasant sex habits.'

'You have a good memory, Mrs Norton.'

'Women have for those sort of things. But don't ever ask me who the Foreign Secretary is. I wouldn't know.'

'So your husband would have met Miss Frail through you?'

A shadow crossed her face. 'How perceptive you are. To my regret, she did. My particular regret in this instance.' She met his sympathetic eyes and bit at her bottom lip. 'He can't help it, Mr Rogers. No more than he can help being besotted with his falconry.' She said wryly, 'If I and one of his birds were in collision, he'd call the vet first and the doctor second.'

'That only means he's a typical Englishman.'

She laughed for the first time. Quietly and for her own

consumption. 'I used to spend my life running round after the blasted things with a shovel and a wet mop. Like an attendant votary round the Sacred Flame,' she said ruminatively. 'No more, though.'

'I noticed you hadn't done the car seats lately.'

She laughed again, sharing it this time. 'So you know what I mean.'

He said carefully, 'I would have thought it understandable had you spread your own wings and flown the coop.'

'I'm a Roman Catholic.' She said it as though it were answer enough.

'It must be pretty wearing on the nerve-ends,' he commented.

'It is. So can you help me?'

He inspected the fingernails of one hand. 'On the evidence I have,' he said at last, his voice neutral, 'I don't believe your husband can be connected with Miss Frail's death. But that's subject to my being wrong. Which I so often am.'

'Thank you,' she said softly.

'Your husband was friendly with Mr Quint?'

She stared at him surprised. 'Yes. Why do you want to know?'

'He also might have known Miss Frail.'

'I believe he used to.' She wasn't intending being very informative about Quint. 'I'm sure you'll be asking him.'

'Don't misunderstand me,' he said, 'but do *you* know him?'

She was cool. 'Slightly. Very slightly. But please don't ask me to talk about him.'

'He has visited here?'

'To draw the birds, yes.'

He said, 'Forgive my saying so but there's a quite surprising resemblance between you and Miss Frail.'

She returned his regard calmly. 'It's not so very surprising, Mr Rogers. She was my cousin.'

Dickersen, president of the High Moor Speleological Society, was a raw-boned man with thick pebble-lensed spectacles and muscular wrists and hands. There were rope burns on the palm he gave to Rogers to shake. He smoked shag tobacco in a cobby pipe. He had offered his rubber pouch to Rogers who, smoking the harsh black mixture with assumed satisfaction, wished he hadn't accepted.

Dickersen's bed-sittingroom was cluttered with the impedimenta of his obsession with caving. There were collapsible aluminium ladders, coils of nylon rope, cord-threaded pitons and a scarred yellow-painted plastic helmet. The walls were decorated with sectionalized scale drawings of caves and fissures.

'It's a hefty-sounding job,' he observed through a cloud of villainous smoke. 'We've only a dozen or so teams. Even when they're all available.'

'I can limit it for you,' Rogers said. He coughed raspingly and laid his pipe aside. Courtesy for him had clearly defined limits. Charring his tongue and epiglottis was outside them. 'The hole I'm looking for should be near to a road. Or if a track, then one capable of being used by a car. And within reasonable distance of the town. Does that help?'

Dickersen went to a table and unrolled a large-scale map. 'It helps,' he said. He studied the map with Rogers at his side. 'If you want them with vertical drops, there's this one, this . . .' He dabbed the stem of his pipe on several red-crayoned rings. 'None of them deeper than a hundred and fifty to the first elbow.'

'Those are the nine possibles?'

'Nine we can start with. None of them much good.

138

Some are virtual craters, some just crevices. Some of them've got water running into them. Cattle and sheep fall down one or two, poor beasties. And that makes for unpleasant climbing. A couple of them have very crumbly pitches. Anyway, it'll take an hour or so in each. How sure are you about this?'

'Not very. But I'd guess more than a fifty-fifty chance.'

'You're assuming the body would have been dropped? Not hauled in?'

'Definitely dropped.'

'Um. A bit sick-making for someone to find.' He flexed his powerful fingers. 'You'll be there, of course?'

'What time do you think you can get started?'

Dickersen blew smoke over the map, then glanced at a clock on the mantelpiece. It was six-thirty. 'By the time I get the lads organized, not much before eight-thirty to nine.'

'I'll be there. Make our Operations Centre here at Blackbeg Rock.' He poked a finger on the map. 'I'll have a couple of communications cars and plenty of lights. And a personal radiophone for each team.'

'If we find something, you'll be going down?'

Rogers grimaced. 'If I have to. But I'm a Grade One claustrophobic. You people must be mad to do it for fun.'

Dickersen looked at him as if he were some grotesque insect. 'You'll love it,' he said with the utter conviction of fanaticism. 'It's a different world underground.'

'I,' Rogers said firmly, 'would prefer to delay the experience until I'm dead.'

Coltart was pacing back and forth outside the main entrance to the headquarters building when Rogers wrestled his car into one of the parking squares marked 'Staff'. The sergeant's usual low-key phlegm seemed to have taken a severe beating.

'I've been looking for you all over,' he rumbled

disapprovingly at Rogers through the window of the car. 'We've located Lingard.'

Rogers pushed open the passenger door. 'Get in,' he snapped. 'Where?'

'The junction of Rooks Hill and Spaniards Rise.' The massive sergeant's entry into the car made it sag and squeak. 'There's a patrol constable keeping tabs on him until we arrive.'

They found Lingard standing in the protection of a high brick wall, making no attempt at concealment. A nearby street lamp threw its loop of dingy yellow light over him, fumid in the encroaching mist. He was in a position where no car could enter or leave Spaniards Rise without his seeing it. Quint's house was about five hundred yards from where Lingard stood and not in view. Spye Green Hall was not a lot further and, had it been daylight, would have been easily visible.

Although Rogers braked the car to a halt almost at his toes, Lingard neither moved nor acknowledged its presence. With Coltart a lumbering shadow behind him, Rogers flicked off the headlights and left the car, facing his former deputy.

This near, he could see the flatness, the emptiness, of the blue eyes. There was none of the amiable, elegant Lingard he had known. In his place was a haggard, grief-eroded stranger with an obsessional hatred burning acid holes in his stomach. His yellow hair was unkempt and he needed a shave. He was without an overcoat, his lightweight suit creased as if he'd made violent love in it. He was unsuccessfully trying not to shiver in the cold night air.

'I'd like you to come to the station for a talk, David,' Rogers began gently. He was warm enough in his fleece-lined car coat and he felt pity for the frozen, delusional Lingard.

The empty eyes turned to his for as long as it took to

say, 'Go away. Leave me alone.' His breath smelled of too many Pernods.

'No. There are questions I have to ask. Questions needing answers from you.' Rogers tried to force the eyes to meet his, to establish contact. 'We can't talk in the road.'

When there was no response, he asked, 'What are you waiting here for, David?'

'Justice,' he answered quietly, almost to himself. 'Now leave me alone.'

'You think you'll get it from Quint? That you'll find it here?'

Lingard did not trouble to reply.

'People taking the law into their own hands are seldom right, David. Police officers, never.'

'No?' There was indifference in the reply.

'What makes you so sure Quint will be returning?'

There was a flicker of uncertainty in Lingard's eyes. 'If I wanted to talk to Quint – or anyone else – I've a right to. I've all the privileges of a normal citizen. One of them being to stand on a pavement and wait. All night if I wish to. *You* say I want to see Quint. You've a right to think what you like. I've a right to refuse to say who I want to see or what I want to do.'

Rogers removed the friendly padding from his manner. 'Why did you quarrel with Miss Frail on Sunday afternoon?'

Lingard's lips thinned. They were livid under the yellow light.

'Was it because you found out she was still married?'

The dead eyes came alive, glowing with a burning anger. His voice shook. 'I warn you, Rogers . . .' He twitched his head and abruptly turned, walking away.

Rogers strode after him, catching him up and clamping his fingers on the narrow shoulders. He swung him around and slammed him hard against the wall. Lingard's breath exploded from his opened mouth and he clenched his hands into fists, holding them against his chest.

Rogers' face was sharp-planed with anger. 'You'll listen to me, David, if I have to knock you unconscious to make you do it.'

Lingard was docile in Rogers' grasp, making no effort to free himself. With his eyes not six inches from Rogers', he said dully, 'You know I could break both your arms if I wanted to.' Which was possibly true. He practised a lethal variant of karate which Rogers had never tested in angry opposition. 'You want me to resist you. So you can arrest me . . .'

Rogers removed his grip from the submissive shoulders. 'Yes, I do,' he growled. 'You should be locked up for your own good.'

Coltart had moved with Rogers and was stolidly waiting on events, his green eyes glittering his interest. He would welcome a personal showdown with the former detective inspector whom he had never liked. Nor did he want Rogers to be selfish about it.

'Tell me why you quarrelled,' Rogers repeated.

'We didn't quarrel,' Lingard said tonelessly. 'I don't know what you're talking about.'

'Why did you drive past her flat at nine-thirty when you were supposed to be keeping observation on the Tico-Tico?'

'I didn't.'

'You're lying, David,' Rogers said sadly.

'If you say I am.'

'You called on Midgley . . .'

'I made no secret of it.'

'You telephoned Mrs Dominis.'

'Did I? *You're* saying all these things.' He took his small ivory snuff box from his waistcoat pocket and with a touch of his former elegance inhaled the tobacco powder. The silk Paisley handkerchief he used was crumpled and dirty and left brown smears on his nostrils.

Rogers cocked his head on one side, measuring Lingard with squeezed-together eyes. 'You've stopped being a copper,' he said sombrely. 'All you've got left is a damn great bellyful of self-pity.' To Rogers, it was like discovering suppurating putrefaction in an apparently healthy leg. He did everything but actually spit. 'All over a bloody woman who wasn't worth it. Who wasn't even faithful to you ...'

Lingard's cheek twitched in his grey face. The taut sinews in his neck showed with how much difficulty he was holding back from throwing himself in a screaming rage at Rogers. Somebody was breathing harshly. It was difficult to decide which of the two men it was.

Coltart's chest rumbled a warning in the background.

Rogers shouted at the blond man. 'Did she take your guts as well!' He prodded at his chest with a rough finger. 'You bloody spineless ninny! A little trouble and you cry your eyes out.'

Whatever it was he expected from Lingard, he didn't get it. Lingard blanked his eyes from his tormentor, scrubbing any expression from his face. His self-control was iron-hard and Rogers bled for him.

When he spoke it was in a tired voice. 'I know why you're saying these things. You want to arrest me. Well, I'm not giving you the excuse.' He added ambiguously, almost as an afterthought, 'I shan't always be so unobliging with you.' For a moment, he was Beau Brummell being aristocratically arrogant with a dunning creditor.

Rogers put away his aggressiveness. 'All right, David. I shall arrange for Sergeant Hagbourne to be here. He'll be instructed to arrest you if you so much as approach Quint. Is that clear?'

143

Lingard regarded him steadily. Then he said politely, 'May I go?'

When he received no reply from Rogers, he turned and walked away down the hill, not looking back, losing himself in the thickening mist.

'What do you make of that?' Rogers asked Coltart.

The sergeant grunted. 'Did you really believe he'd have a go at you?'

'I was as nasty a bastard as I dared be. Too nasty and his arrest wouldn't have stuck for five minutes. Undue provocation or somesuch.'

'He's got a thing about Quint.'

'If Quint's still about, I think Lingard could be mad enough to kill him. Given the right stimulus. And knowing how bloody-minded Quint can be, he'd give it to him.'

'But you don't know if Quint *is* about.'

Rogers bared his wrist watch of two inches of soiled shirt cuff. 'Ask me in a couple of hours' time,' he said.

12

Hacker hadn't been difficult for Rogers to locate. He was knocking golf balls with a No 2 wood at the Sporting Club's indoor driving range.

Rogers waited at one side while he drove at the canvas bull's-eye wired to the netting at the far end of the floodlit shed.

'I've been expecting you,' the optician said with a cheerful grin over his shoulder.

He was a handsome slim man with crinkly black hair. He wore a red crewneck pullover with white linen trousers and rubber spiked shoes. He gripped a thick unlit havana between his teeth and spoke around it. 'I hear in the bazaars you're getting all hot and bothered about Nancy.' The amiability that reached his spectacled eyes was strictly the small change of social intercourse.

'I'm not putting you off your stroke?' Rogers asked sardonically as Hacker teed a ball and waggled the club head behind it.

'No. I always practise my shots with coppers asking me questions.' The club swung up, paused and slashed down, sending the ball whistling towards the left of the target. 'I'm bloody useless with a two wood,' he muttered. 'I hook like hell with it.'

He put an arm around Rogers' shoulders and squeezed, showing his gleaming porcelain smile. 'Don't take any notice of what I say. I *like* coppers. You're all that stands between us lambs and anarchy and our being up shit creek.'

'I'm glad to hear it,' the unresponsive Rogers said, disengaging from the embrace. He didn't like being handled by another man.

'Some of my best friends are coppers.'

'And you'd let your sister marry one?'

Hacker looked blank. 'My sister . . . ?'

'A joke,' Rogers said dourly. 'It's supposed to be the acid test of sincerity.' Beneath the spurious bonhomie, both men were willing to dish out punishment.

'Ha! Ha! I see it now. Very funny.' Hacker squinted along the length of the club. 'You want to know about me and Nancy?'

'More or less.'

He reached down, teeing the ball carefully and precisely. Straightening himself, he said, 'It was a simple pay-as-you-enter relationship. Which you probably know already or you wouldn't be here. I won't give you any guff about lonely hearts and similar crap. A man can't help the dynamo of his testicles and he's got to do

145

something about it. And to put it crudely, my dear chap, what Nancy had between her legs was a fur-lined cash register.' He lifted the club and whipped it down with a slashing motion, topping the ball and sending it scuttling crablike over the peat-strewn floor. Hacker swore.

'You dipped your left shoulder on the back swing,' Rogers commented, giving his unwanted opinion. 'Miss Frail. She was worth it?'

'Nancy? God, yes. The ultimate experience. With nothing barred, although she could spit and claw like a wild cat when the mood took her.' He wagged his head. Even with the odd-looking spectacles he wore, Rogers considered him too pretty for his approval. 'She liked her pleasures on the crude side. But money mad . . .'

'When did you last see her?'

'Sunday week. The fifth, I think it was.'

'At her flat?'

'Yes.'

'Had you ever noticed a painting there? A cat and three female figures?'

Hacker looked cautious. 'Has it been stolen?'

'You did see it then?'

He nodded. 'I remember the cat vaguely, the females distinctly. They all had little purple flowers painted over the interesting parts of their titties. And palm leaves over their whatsisnames.'

'You seem to have had a good look.' Rogers smiled inside at the man.

'Of course I did. I'm a post-graduate student of exotic porn. It makes a change from optometry.' He teed another ball, straightened and snapped a butane gas lighter at his cigar. 'I always relax after making a balls-up of a shot,' he said. 'Oh, yes. I nearly forgot. He raped her once.'

'Jolly good,' Rogers grunted. 'Who raped whom?'

'Her husband. Dominis. He raped Nancy.'

'You were looking through the keyhole?'

Hacker regarded him with faint mockery. 'She told me. And she had a gorgeous shiner under one eye to prove it.'

'How long ago was all this?'

Hacker removed the cigar and pursed his lips. 'Seven or eight weeks. About. I can't be certain.'

'You believed her?'

He held the cigar out to Rogers. 'Would you mind awfully, old chap?'

Rogers took the cigar. The rich leaf was smooth as satin between his finger and thumb, the perfume of the smoke reminiscent of a cooking cabbage.

Hacker drove the ball hard and straight and he smiled. In his mind the ball had represented Rogers. 'Believe her?' He retrieved the cigar from the detective. 'Not altogether. But then I don't believe much of anything women tell me.'

'She didn't report it to the police. I'd have known.'

'Of course she didn't.' Hacker looked amused. 'I expect she enjoyed it. She was that sort of a bitch. It's a compliment to a woman to want her so badly you are prepared to rape her to get it. The law should be amended to allow for this fundamental truth.'

'I'll mention it to the Home Secretary the next time I see him,' Rogers said drily. He added, 'I think she was a liar.'

'So? I was interested in her sex. Not her semantics.'

'You knew Dominis?'

'No. But I damn nearly did.' He threw back his head and laughed, showing his beautiful teeth. 'Some time last December I think it was. Nancy was at my place over the shop. She looked out the window and saw him skulking on the other side of the street. He looked a right mean bastard. Likely to take a dim view of the whole thing. So she didn't leave and we had a ball of a night while we waited for him to go. Which was when it started to get light.' He sucked ruefully at his back teeth. 'That's the night that cost me the contact lenses. It's funny. Although she was badly myopic she could still recognize a ten-pound note at a hundred paces.' He raised his eyes to the polystyrene ceiling. 'Christ! I must have been mad!'

'Yes,' Rogers agreed. 'Did she trust you with a key to her flat?'

He shook his head. 'I didn't need one. All I had to do was to knock twice and make a noise like a well-filled wallet.'

'Do you know anything about her other playmates?'

Hacker glanced at him slyly. 'She mentioned an item or two about her detective boy-friend. None of it very flattering. She told me he had developed into the most monumental bore imaginable. That he amused her in the beginning but took her much too seriously.' He smirked. 'A brighter-than-white knight and incredibly naive . . .'

Rogers cleared his throat, his face stiffening.

Hacker grinned maliciously. 'You asked me.'

'Go on.'

'She said she wasn't used to being treated like someone's grandmother. He was too respectful, too deferential. It made her feel as old as the hills. She used to call him her "cucumber-sandwich-and-tea-on-the-vicarage-lawn man". Behind his back, naturally.' He guffawed. 'He should've taken a lesson from me and treated her like something escaped from the Casbah. She loved it.'

'I can imagine it,' Rogers said coldly. 'The pair of you must have been a rare giggle.'

Hacker wrinkled his nose at the cigar. 'Jealousy'll get you nowhere.' That was the second time it had been said to Rogers and it scratched at his *amour-propre*. Hacker continued, 'Are we going to talk about Lingard or me?'

'Stick to Lingard,' Rogers growled. Without the extraneous comments. He wouldn't appreciate your advice on sex matters.'

'Charming man,' Hacker murmured. 'Anyway, when she realized he was serious . . . on a copper's salary . . .' He laughed, his eyes creased and wicked when he saw Rogers glower. 'She said it wouldn't keep her cats in sardines and milk. So she tried to lose him. But marrying him . . . ?' He sniggered this time.

The detective was sour. 'She'd have raised her status considerably. Lingard was streets ahead of the deprived rubbish she pandered to.' His face was expressionless. 'Present company excepted, of course.' He didn't mean the exception and it showed.

Hacker, smiling with stiff lips, rammed the club back in his bag and selected a murderous No 3 iron. He made a few preliminary swings with it. 'Kind of you, my dear chap. Have you finished? I'm busy.'

'Whose bosoms were you inspecting last Sunday evening?'

Hacker laughed in the detective's face. 'A married woman's. Seventeen miles away in a north-easterly direction. At the Acey-Deucey Club in point of fact. I returned at two in the morning. If you ask her nice and discreetly she'll no doubt confirm it.'

'She'll need to. Who is she?'

Hacker gave him her name and address. Rogers said, 'I'll know her by the free spectacles, I suppose?'

The optician ignored the jibe. 'Her old man's on a permanent night-shift at the steel pressing works. So see her when he's not about to cause trouble.' He regarded Rogers with distrust plain in his eyes. 'And no dipping your spoon in my private jar of honey,' he warned him, not wholly humorously.

Rogers sneered. 'Not even using a disinfected fencing post.' It wasn't brilliant – not even passable – repartee but the best he could do against a man already engrossed in the contemplation of his next shot and who had plainly lost interest in him.

The road glistened like moist liquorice in the headlights of Rogers' car as it climbed into the smoking grey fog of the moors. Below him, resembling burning sulphur gases in a pit, was the vague yellow glow of the town he had just left.

He pulled into the lay-by where Dickersen, standing near the police communications car, was adding the acrid fumes of his pipe tobacco to the fog. The smoke hung around his head like small dabs of cottonwool with nowhere to go. He held his plastic helmet in one hand. Despite the cold he wore only a denim boilersuit over his trousers and shirt. He carried a folder of papers under one arm.

Coltart was with him, bulking large against his stocky companion. A radio transmitter and receiver stood on the bonnet of the car near them. An occasional disembodied voice floated out from it giving the location of the speaker in his descent into the moor's catacombs.

'All the lads are climbing,' Dickersen said to Rogers. He looked at his watch. 'We cleared the first – Lugs Bottom – about five minutes ago.' His words dropped like pieces of wet felt in the waterlogging mist.

Coltart rumbled, 'I've posted a CID man on top of each of the holes for liaison.' To Dickersen, he said, 'Excuse me a moment,' and led Rogers to one side, taking the radio set with him.

'Hagbourne's sitting on Quint's doorstep. Do you want a situation report?'

'I'll talk to him.'

Coltart's banana thumb depressed a button on the transmitter and he spoke, his bass voice vibrating the grille in its side. 'Foxtrot One calling Foxtrot Ten. Are you there?'

Rogers heard a glum-sounding Hagbourne answering and took the set from Coltart. 'Is there any sign of L?' he asked.

'No. But the fog's so thick he'd have to be sitting on my lap before I could see him.'

'And Q?'

'No sign either. And I'm out of cigarettes.'

'That's terrible. Where are you?'

'Inside the gates. On wet turf and beginning to take root.'

'Keep in touch, sergeant.' He added unsympathetically, 'And try chewing grass.'

He handed the set back to Coltart and shivered. The fog swirled around the two men, silvering their hair and the fibres of their clothing. Rogers filled his pipe before returning to Dickersen and the possibility of being offered his pouch of poisonous shag.

The news he waited for came at nine-fifty from the hole known as The Gawp Gut. The climber calling in sounded sick, telling Dickersen he was coming up to the untainted air of topside before he actually was.

The Gawp Gut was less than half-a-mile away. Rogers made it in just over fifty seconds in a blind-eyed drive through the dark muffling fog that had Coltart and Dickersen pressing their feet unhappily on imaginary brake pedals.

A pallid-faced youth wearing a red helmet was sitting on the pit edge with his head cupped in his hands. His companion was massaging the back of his neck.

Rogers walked to him across the soaking clumps of moor grass. 'Are you all right?' he asked.

'No. Anything but.' He grimaced and blinked. 'If I think about it, I shall chuck up.'

'Think just a little bit. What was he like?'

The pallid youth swallowed. 'I didn't stay to look. All I could see was a pair of legs sticking up from inside a dead sheep . . .' He twisted his head to one side and quietly vomited.

When he had finished and was wiping his bloodless lips with a handkerchief, Dickersen asked, 'Where was he, Mike?'

Mike gulped. 'At the bottom of the trough on the second stage.'

Dickersen nodded. He snapped on his helmet light, unfastened the folder he was carrying and selected a plan, holding it open for Rogers to see. It showed The Gawp Gut in section, shaped like a short two-angled fall pipe. After a vertical drop to an elbow, the cave sloped steeply to a level watercourse.

Dickersen indicated the first angle with his forefinger. 'The body would have hit the ledge here on the second stage, bounced off and slithered down the trough to where it's now resting.'

'How deep?' Rogers asked.

'Thirty-eight feet straight down to the first stage. We'll use Mike's ladder. That's kid's stuff. Then a rope-down through the trough for about sixty.' He smiled encouragingly. 'Old ladies have done it blindfolded.'

'Will I need an umbrella?' Rogers asked sarcastically.

'Not in this one. It's a dry run except when it rains. And if it does while we're down there, we'll be washed away like matchsticks in a drain.' He fastened a rope around the detective's waist. 'Keep that on while you're using the ladder.' He indicated Rogers' gloved hands. 'You won't want those. Not with wet nylon.'

'It's only a bloody ladder,' Rogers said impatiently. 'I've climbed them before. Up *and* down.' This particular ladder hung down into a yawning, unattractive blackness but Rogers refused to be intimidated by its apparent flimsiness.

'Maybe you'll find it a queerer ladder than you bargain for.' Dickersen lowered himself over the edge feet first, feeling with his toes for the aluminium rungs. Then he vanished, the ladder jerking with each step he took, only the reflection of his helmet lamp showing his progress.

His voice came up diminished by distance and thinned by enclosing rock. Rogers, his head squeezed into the sick youth's helmet, clambered on to the ladder and stepped downwards into the blackness, his pipe clenched between his teeth. Coltart held the safety rope, playing it out as Rogers descended.

The ladder was, indeed, as queer as Dickersen had warned although he was holding it as taut as Rogers' weight would allow him from below. It swivelled and lurched sideways under the detective's feet with unpredictable malice, skinning the knuckles of his fists wrapped round the white nylon side ropes and scraping the toes of his black oxfords. His stomach felt wobbly and he remembered he hadn't eaten anything since his sandwiches at Henri et Camille's. As he dropped down, so the wet grey stone slid upwards six inches from his nose in the disc of light from the lamp on his helmet. When he tilted his head he could see the vanishing perspective of his safety rope, metal rungs and distorted shadows. He didn't care to look down between his feet.

When he thought he must be getting short of ladder, he felt Dickersen tap his heels and heard him say, 'Six more rungs,' and after that finding himself balancing on a ledge big enough for two small chickens. A passage about four feet in diameter fell away below.

Dickersen's eyes glinted behind the pebble lenses. 'You OK?'

Rogers grunted. 'Apart from running out of skin on my fingers, yes.'

Dickersen untied Rogers' safety rope and knotted it to a steel piton already hammered into the rock face. 'Watch me carefully,' he said. He manœuvred the rope between his thighs, around his buttocks and over a shoulder, allowing the tail of it to drop into the hole behind him. 'Let it slide between your hands,' he instructed. 'Like this.' He walked backwards down the steep trough of the passage, crouching to avoid the roof.

When the rope slackened, Rogers heard his faint words echoing up from the depths. 'Hurry up. There's not much room for the three of us.'

'Three?' Rogers called the word into the passage.

'Don't forget the sheep. It takes up a lot of room.'

Rogers, fitting the rope around his body, backed down the slope, the nylon burning his hands, his wrists aching from the strain. Warm-blooded humanity on topside seemed a long hour away from him. He was entombed in a hostile, suffocating and silent world. He swallowed his spit, wanting nothing more than the moral courage to scramble back up the ladder like a sensibly scared rabbit. His claustrophobic imagination made the walls tumble in on him in slow motion. He thought deliberately of a fleshy Bridget in his arms in an effort to take the sick foreboding from his fears.

Once he slipped, swivelling on his back, his heels scrabbling frantically on the rock for purchase and he had a horrifying picture of tumbling into the decaying flesh below. He pulled himself upright again and sweated. He imagined he could already smell its putrefaction.

Dickersen held his ankles and guided his feet as he reached the debris of small stones at the bottom. There was a gurgling of running water and the small sounds of their movement echoed. 'A born caver,' Dickersen said laconically. 'I'll get you enrolled as a member when we get back.'

'*If* we get back,' Rogers growled. 'This is my first and last time.' His nostrils twitched as the smell of corruption reached them with its evil miasma. 'For God's sake,' he said, 'smoke some of that tobacco of yours. Anything's preferable.'

He filled his own pipe as he studied the body at his feet. Dominis was not instantly recognizable. His head was buried in the distended belly of a dead sheep, his legs unnaturally and grotesquely twisted. One hand, held out appealingly, was frozen with bent fingers in their last grasp at the something they had never reached. The dark blue coat was rucked up over the hips, showing a blood-soaked pullover. The pale blue trousers were concertinad to expose livid shins.

Rogers disliked handling dead flesh and he used a handkerchief over his fingers to twist the torn face out from its fleece pillow; to recognize the lady-killing moustache and the AFC scar on the left temple; to see the dreadful fixed stare of violent death and the dried blood fouling the chin and necktie.

'He's the one you were looking for?' Dickersen asked.

'Yes, poor bastard. The prototype Do-It-Yourself private detective. He should have left it to the professionals.'

13

It took nearly an hour of grunting, straining effort at the ropes to haul up the stretcher to which the body of Dominis had been lashed.

Rogers stood with Bridget on the rim of the dark hole of The Gawp Gut. A semi-circle of hissing butane lamps poured hot beams of diffused light on to the stretcher being manœuvred over the outcrop lip on to level ground.

Bridget, pulling on rubber gloves, said lightly, 'I hope you'll come as quickly when I whistle for *you*, George. I thought you'd lost my number.'

He stared into the orange of her eyes. 'A temporary amnesia. Events have been scything my legs from beneath me.'

'Along with David's?'

'Yes,' he said gloomily. 'You know?'

She nodded. 'He's in trouble?'

'He could be.'

'I'm sorry. He's a nice boy.'

'He's also a fool.'

She turned towards the body, now isolated on a square of polythene, and said casually, 'Talking of fools, don't forget you didn't finish your sherry.'

The pressure was on and Rogers realized with sudden clarity that there was rarely a single watershed. They came in pluralities. He thought he'd cross this particular one when he walked into it.

He stood behind her with Coltart and Dickersen and a small group of emerged potholers forming a silent semi-circle, watching her deft fingers examining Dominis's face, hooking a finger inside the mouth, lifting up the eyelids. She paused in her scrutiny of the lacerated forehead, picking out a granule of crystal from the bloodied flesh with a pair of tweezers.

She held it out to Rogers. 'Windscreen glass?'

He looked closely at it and nodded. 'It fits the wobbly sort of theory I have.'

She unbuttoned and unzipped the dead man's clothing, exclaiming a soft 'Agh' of satisfaction when she pulled the shirt up and bared the dreadfully mangled stomach. She pressed it with the pads of her fingers.

156

The men watching moved uneasily for Dominis's mouth had opened in what looked like a soundless yell. Rogers smiled grimly when he saw Dickersen edge backwards out of the group, his face tallow-coloured.

'Gross crushing injuries to the abdomen,' Bridget said without looking up. 'Consistent with having been run over by a car. He must have died almost immediately.'

'Does the time of death fit in with our other problem?'

She flexed an arm and then a leg. 'Yes. Very roughly forty-eight hours. But don't hold it against me. It needs some higher mathematics in the mortuary.' She lowered her voice. 'He was with her?'

'Yes. But not necessarily inside the car. And the little I know is more about the How than the Why. I'm being lied to, of course.'

'Of course,' she agreed, standing and stripping her hands of the gloves. 'Isn't that the cross a policeman is always nailed to?'

'Yes. But more understandable when lied to by the guilty than by the presumably innocent.'

He crouched at the side of the corpse. 'No tyre marks on the clothing,' he commented to Coltart. 'That should mean something to me but doesn't. And no more bits of windscreen glass that I can see.' He straightened his legs and beat his hands together. The fog was freezing all his previous sweating out of him. 'Get Dr Dagg up here, sergeant. I'd like him to run his vacuum cleaner over the clothing before it's moved.'

To Bridget, he said, 'Can you do your examination first thing in the morning?'

She nodded. 'Tonight if you like. But the answer's going to be death due to crushing injuries.'

'No,' he said. 'Do it tomorrow morning. I'm walking on my chin strap already.'

She stared at him hard, her eyes bright. 'Telephone me

157

about it later,' she said softly. 'I keep a stock of spare chin straps.'

A faint voice, querulous and demanding, came from Coltart's coat pocket. He dragged the radio out, bringing most of the lining with it. Hagbourne's voice became clear, asking for Rogers. 'Quint,' he said when Rogers answered him. 'He pulled into the drive in his Rolls a few minutes ago. He's now in the house.'

'No sign of L?'

'I wouldn't guarantee it,' Hagbourne replied pessimistically. 'This bloody fog! I haven't seen the ends of my legs since I came up here.'

'Do you know what Quint's up to?'

'Yes. I peeked through the window. He's been talking on the telephone since he arrived.'

'How does he look?'

'Worried.'

'Go and sit with him,' Rogers said. 'I'll be over in a few minutes. Talk to him, tell him jokes, do anything. But keep the . . .'

'Just a minute, sir . . .' Rogers heard the click of Hagbourne's thumb pressure being released.

He waited, hearing only the crackle and hiss of static. 'What is it, sergeant?' he asked sharply. 'Sergeant! Sergeant Hagbourne!' He stared at the mute set, his face grim. Then he tossed it at Coltart. 'Stay here and look after things,' he said, already running.

His car shuddered as he slammed the door and took off, accelerating downhill with the tyres rasping rubber on the chipping-surfaced road.

With his nose to the windscreen and the wipers clacking, he blundered into the blank wall of fog at a dangerous speed, alternately accelerating and braking. Twice, blinded by the headlights of approaching vehicles, he swerved, gouging lumps of earth and grass from the verge.

When he finally reached the street lamps of Rooks Hill he was livid with frustration.

Turning into Spaniards Rise, he killed his engine and coasted silently on side lights to the gates of the Old Rectory, jumping out almost before the car came to a halt.

Hagbourne, his eyes protuberant with effort, had his shoulder-blades against the angle of one of the gate pillars, rubbing at the necktie binding his arms behind him. His radio lay on the gravel at his feet.

Rogers cut the tie with his pocketknife and the sergeant spat out a gobbet of blood. 'He's mad,' he gasped, rubbing the side of his throat. 'He came from around the wall and clobbered me.' He held his head lopsided, looking at Rogers' angry face. 'I'm sorry. I didn't expect him to hit me like that . . . no warning . . .'

'It's done,' Rogers said shortly. 'We'll argue about it later. I only hope I'm in time to stop him.'

Hagbourne spat blood again. 'This time I'll be ready.'

'No you won't. This time you stay here and make sure he doesn't get out. If he's still in there, that is. Use that radio of yours and get some assistance here.'

He saw there were lights in the lower rooms of the house as he ran up the stone steps. He opened the door and stepped into the dark hall. It was as cold in there as it was outside.

He recognized Lingard's voice behind a closed door. Although muffled by the heavy wood, it was sharp and vicious and what he said was answered by a groan. Rogers pressed down on the handle of the door and pushed. It remained solid and immovable. The groan came again and, on the heels of it, the sound of the smacking of flesh on flesh.

Rogers depressed the handle again and heaved his bulk against the door. The impact shook him to the marrow and rattled his teeth but the door remained solid. There were sounds of hasty movement behind it and a thud as he drew back and slammed the flat of his foot jarringly on the lock. With a splintering crash the door exploded inwards.

Quint, his face blotched and swollen, lay on his back. The door behind him was open. Rogers reached him in a few quick strides. The cream-haired man was staring vacantly at the ceiling and bubbling saliva, his breathing stertorous. One arm was twisted beneath his body. He groaned. To Rogers, it was a reassuring sound. A slim green-leafed cigar burned on the carpet at Quint's side and Rogers put his foot on it.

The open door led to the arboretum. Rogers knew its interior well. There was a short windowless passage and then a further safety door to the mini-jungle of tropical greenery. Four months ago it had been a steam-heated Mato Grosso, alive with exotic birds, lizards and frogs: swarming with the mosquitoes and fruit flies bred in their myriads to feed them.

He walked quietly along the passage. The door at its far end was ajar. He paused, pushing it wide open. It led to the enormous metal-ribbed structure towering dimly to the black sky. The reflected glow from the lamp outside in the road gave the interior an ochre luminosity. A giant tree fern stood in dark silhouette with its topmost fronds thirty feet above the ground. It was surrounded by palms and tall bamboos hung with creepers and hairy mosses. The shrubbery had grown rank and wild. There was a life-lessness and dankness in there with the pervasive smell of decaying vegetation. Fog billowed in through the broken panes of glass and torn lining of polythene.

For the second time that evening, Rogers felt himself in alien territory, away from his ordered and familiar world of stone and brick and tarmac. Here he sensed very strongly the menace of shadowed foliage and the feeling of being watched by a hunting animal.

He groped silently with his fingers for the switches on the wall and snapped them on. Nothing happened and he swore inside his mind.

'David?' He spoke conversationally. 'I know you're in there.'

There was a remote rustle of sound, so soft it might have been the pulsing of his own blood through his arteries. He suddenly felt old and tired and useless; his body aching from his climb into The Gawp Gut. His knuckles were raw and smarting and he thought that fighting even an ailing pygmy shrew might be beyond him. 'You can't get out,' he continued. 'Only this way. And I'm here.'

The quiet cold voice from the other side of the trees said, 'I'm going out. Please don't try and stop me.'

'I'm arresting you, David.' Rogers shifted his position, stepping forward into the arboretum. He turned his coat collar up, covering the whiteness of his shirt. 'You've forgotten everything a police officer should remember.'

'I'm not a police officer.' He wasn't making a point, just saying it. 'I resigned.'

'Does that stop your being fair? You were acting on the level of a street-corner lout.' There was cutting contempt in the words. 'You were trying to beat an admission out of him.'

'Pussyfoot Rogers,' the voice said tightly.

'Not so pussyfoot I can't take you, David.'

'You'll have to. You took me by surprise last time.'

Rogers moved forward two silent paces on the flag-stoned path. 'Like you did with Hagbourne?'

There was a faint shirring of disturbed leaves and Lingard's words came from a different angle. 'Did I hurt him?' There was no anxiety, no curiosity, in the question.

'Enough.'

In the still, unbreathing silence, Rogers' hearing seemed unnaturally acute. He could hear tiny scratching noises he thought to be mice or insects. Somewhere above him water bubbled in one of the metal pipes used to provide the storms the miniature rain-forest needed.

There were pots of dried-up shrubs at his feet. He manipulated one pot between his shoes and slowly, not breathing, grasped its stem and pulled the plant out with its ball of soil intact. Against Lingard's undoubted adequacy at karate and his theoretical ability to kill by it, Rogers needed something more devastating than muscle, something less obvious than his own elementary knowledge of judo. He judged a lump of solid earth, swung accurately at the end of the shrub, might be it. That and jolting Lingard from his inhuman iciness: making him lose his temper.

Lingard spoke out of the darkness. He was appreciably nearer. 'Let me go out of the door. I don't want to fight you.'

Rogers answered that by ignoring it. 'Why did you pick on Quint?'

Lingard was a long time silent. Then he said, 'You know why. Because he killed Nancy.'

'There was no murder and you know it.'

'There are other ways. Not in the book. Things . . . just as bad. He was with her that night.'

There was a soft contempt in Rogers' voice. 'So Midgley said. But that doesn't make it so. It could have been one of six others.' He remembered the late Lieutenant Colonel Jagger and the crippled Garwood. 'Well four, anyway.'

There was a ghost of movement from near the trunk of the giant fern. Rogers strained his eyes but could see only a confusion of dark shapes. He stepped sideways on to the peat soil, his shoes sinking deep into it.

'You heard me, David?' He was like a bat: sending words winging into the darkness that had their echoes in movement or sound.

'I heard you.' The articulation had the precision of polished steel balls. 'She was far above your grimy understanding.'

'You're deceiving yourself, David. Deliberately and against all the evidence. You know she was married twice?'

'*Liar.*' It wasn't much above a whisper.

'All right. I'm a liar. But hear me out. The first was to an American, Eugene Swerdloff. Does that mean anything to you?' His scalp tingled and his leg muscles ached with holding himself motionless. There were small, fragmentary sounds of movement around him. Water dripped on leaves somewhere, distracting his attention from keeping Lingard located. 'We've found Dominis. He was murdered.'

'The filthy pawing bastard. He deserved it.'

That came from behind him and Rogers turned slightly. Now he daren't stir. His only remaining move was out into the open and there he would be exposed. He had to draw Lingard to him. 'You're a paranoic, David. You need help...treatment.'

There was a noise outside of tyres crunching over gravel and the glaring beams of a car's headlights swept across the arboretum, elongating shadows and sending them racing, piercing the gloom with sudden shafts of blinding light. Then there was darkness again, followed by the clunking of metal doors and approaching footsteps.

Rogers guessed he had been seen. 'I'll repeat what I said before,' he rasped cruelly, bracing himself to swing his soil bludgeon. 'She was the Great Whore of Babylon. Opening her legs to anybody with a fistful of pound notes.'

He heard a sharp intake of breath at one side of him. Very much nearer now.

'Why don't you face up to facts . . .'

There came a soft whisper of the scraping of papery leaves, a displacement of air and Lingard was suddenly in front of him, his shadowed face murderous. A hissing noise came from between his teeth as he moved fluidly with the grace and rhythm of a striking snake, ducking his head and twisting his body, flashing an upward-curving kick at Rogers' jaw. Rogers flung himself sideways as the sole of the shoe slammed into his shoulder, spinning him backwards into the bush. At the same time, he swung desperately with the clod of earth, feeling it disintegrate against Lingard's cheekbone as he followed up his attack. It was a staggering blow but no more than enough to check him momentarily.

Rogers experienced a blighting spasm of paralysing fear. This was a Lingard he had never known or suspected. Completely berserk, his blows were being delivered with savage ferocity. Rogers, helpless in the tangling branches, covered up as Lingard chopped at him. He grasped a fistful of Lingard's jacket and pulled him down, his free arm taking the numbing blows. He jolted an elbow into Lingard's stomach and heard him gasp, smelling the Pernod and snuff on his breath. He was making growling noises, worrying at him like a mad dog.

Rogers, his arm aching from the punishment it was receiving, realized clearly that if the younger man succeeded in hitting him in the right place on his throat he would choke and die. That was when desperation gave him a viciousness of his own. With his arms tangling Lingard's efforts to get in a finishing blow, he drove his knee piston hard into the squashiness of his genitals. Although Lingard screamed hoarsely like a tortured animal, he continued his chopping, his ferocity diamond-

164

hard. The cutting edge of his palm struck fire into the side of Rogers' neck, bringing tears to his eyes. He grunted and wrapped his arms bear-like around Lingard, pulling him down and snapping his own skull violently into the nose of his opponent. Feeling the abrupt relaxation of muscles, he balled a fist and drove it with a solid smack against the jaw exposed above him; a blow that flung Lingard across his legs in a sudden boneless collapse.

Panting harshly, Rogers pulled free from beneath him, grasping and twisting his arms behind his back. He knelt one knee on them, wrenching his handcuffs from a pocket and clipping them on the unresisting wrists.

Lingard's eyes were agonized in his soil-covered face, his nose pumping blood over his mouth and chin. When Rogers hoisted him upright he bowed his head and stood abject with shaking legs.

'I'm sorry, David,' Rogers said gently. 'I would have liked to have left you with your illusions. I can't see you've got anything else.'

14

Quint, slumped on a yellow plush chaise-longue, was being nursemaided by a uniformed constable. Still dazed and with one boiled-egg eye he had seen the handcuffed Lingard escorted from the arboretum by Hagbourne and the driver of the patrol car. Rogers stood waiting while the constable practised a rudimentary first-aid on Quint's arm, slinging it in two handkerchiefs knotted together. Occasionally Quint groaned and closed his eyes. He wasn't very anxious to talk to Rogers.

When he had been suitably prepared for later treatment by a doctor, Rogers jerked his head at the constable, telling him to leave. It was cold in the room and he kicked down the switch of an electric fire, moving it closer to Quint. The house had an unlived-in air about it. He opened a lacquered box on a table and took out a spinach-green cigar. 'A smoke?' he asked.

Quint nodded and Rogers pushed it between the swollen lips, holding a match to it. Then he lit his pipe, tamping down the burning shreds of tobacco with a fingertip long inured to incineration. While he did so he studied Quint.

Four months hadn't changed him. His creamy-blond hair still possessed the contrived shagginess of a middle-aged male interested in women; his skin still golden from regular exposure to a sun-tan lamp. He was lean and sinewy in his carefully tailored tweed suit. His apricot shirt, torn at the throat and with a button missing, was hand sewn with a high collar and four-inch cuffs. The knitted brown tie had been torn loose.

Beneath its lumpiness, his face was raffish and handsome with lids hooding secretive pale eyes. The thin arrogant nose was nostrilled with the miniature cheeks of a belly-dancer's buttocks, each possessing an astonishing mobility of its own. He was the sort of man whom other men, owning to bored wives, eyed warily and wished impotent or somewhere else.

'Don't tell me this sudden concern for my comfort is altruistic,' he said with sour mockery.

Rogers smiled with his lips together. 'I'm cold too. I'd rather ask my questions in comfort.' He pulled a chair nearer to Quint and sat facing him. 'A doctor'll be here soon. In the meantime, you're fit enough?'

Quint released smoke from his mouth as if he hadn't the strength to blow it. 'There's nothing wrong with me that a month in hospital and a bonesetter won't cure,' he said nastily. 'To be honest, I'd hoped to have seen the last of you.' He winced and touched the side of his jaw with a fingertip. 'The bastard! He was as unstable as an elephant in *must*.'

'And for much the same reason.' Rogers stared at him with the unwinking regard of a policeman. 'He didn't approve of your association with Nancy Frail.'

'So he said.'

Rogers was earnest. 'I want you to know he wasn't acting as a police officer. He'd resigned.'

'He told me that too. Before he started knocking me about. Which was bloody considerate of him. It made a difference.'

'You knew why he was like it?'

'He didn't go into details. A mere matter of accusing me of being responsible for her death . . . of raping her.' His lips twisted in a humourless grin. 'Raping *her*! My God. He had to be joking.'

'No, he wasn't. To the deluded, all things are delusional. And they insist on ramming their delusions down other people's throats. Perhaps his knowing you were at her flat on Sunday evening had something to do with it.'

Quint examined the lengthening ash of his cigar and adjusted his arm in its sling.

When he didn't answer, Rogers said patiently, 'That was a sort of question, Mr Quint. What were you doing there at nine o'clock that evening?'

'I don't remember saying I was there, chief inspector.'

He knew this form of patronising address would irritate Rogers and it did. 'You're saying you weren't?' His shoulders and neck throbbed painfully, not improving a disposition that was never very merry at the best of times.

Quint held the cigar to his mouth and spoke around it. 'That's something you'll have to prove.' He blew smoke. 'If you can.' It was an act. Despite his nonchalance he was beginning to look worried.

'All right. Would the sighting of an old black Rolls-

Royce car with a woman passenger and a Photo-fit picture by an eye-witness of a middle-aged six-footer with fair hair be enough?'

Although his fingers had jerked ash from the cigar on to his shirt front, he answered calmly enough. 'If you ask the Rolls-Royce people I expect you'll find they've built more than one black Phantom Five in their time.' He pursed his pulpy lips. 'And I vaguely recollect there exist a few other tall men with fair hair.'

Rogers smiled tightly. 'The self-delusory confidence of the layman. It's sustained some of them even on the gallows' trap. So don't lean too heavily on it. What were you doing there?'

Quint shook his head stubbornly. His tan had turned blotchy.

'There's another fallacy,' Rogers commented mildly, 'that if you say "no" enough times, a policeman will believe you and go away. You're dodging the issue,' he said sternly. 'And because you're dodging it, I know you've something to hide. And knowing that . . .' He showed his teeth. '. . . your movements and statements deserve close scrutiny. Who was the woman with you?'

Quint grimaced. 'If I knew a socially acceptable way of telling you to get stuffed, I'd say it.'

Rogers smiled. It was the sort of smile more fraught with danger than another man's scowl. 'Lingard thought it was Nancy Frail.'

'Assuming – just assuming, mind you – I was with a woman, I can assure you it wouldn't have been Nancy.'

'And if it had, you wouldn't admit it anyway?'

'You're clairvoyant.'

'When did you see her last?'

Quint hesitated. 'Back in June. Not since.'

'You're sure about that?' He stared hard at him. Quint was held by his continued scrutiny. Rogers knew it to be an unnerving experience to be the object of another's unblinking regard. Quint was standing up to it well.

'I'm sure.'

'I don't understand why.'

'Why I'm sure?'

'No. Why you stopped being a paying customer.'

Patches of pink showed on Quint's cheeks. 'You've a singularly nasty way of putting things, Rogers.'

'So I've been told. At five pounds a coupling why should you complain of a little indelicacy in my describing it? Why did you stop?'

'I got bored.' He brushed cigar ash from his trousers on to the carpet. 'Much as I am now.'

'Or you met someone else.' Rogers noted the flicker in his eyes.

Quint's nostrils did their little belly dance of agitation but he only shook his head.

'Where have you been since Sunday?'

'I don't see that's any of your business.'

Rogers sighed. 'You don't know how many people have said that to me and how many times I've had to insist it is. Tell me, please. Where?'

'I don't suppose it matters. London. Room forty-two at The Tudor Court Hotel in Cromwell Road. It's within staggering distance of The British Museum of Natural History.'

'You drove there?'

'I caught the ten twenty-seven train Monday morning.'

'And your car?'

'I parked it on the station approach.'

'You went with your wife?' He could guess the answer to that.

'My wife,' he replied stiffly, 'left me after that last effort of yours about her brother.'

'You aren't blaming me?' Rogers bristled. He had so

very nearly bedded with Judith that he was touchy about it.

'No. But then, I'm not thanking you either.'

'You were on your own?'

'Yes.'

'Doing what?' With Quint being so unusually forthcoming, he knew the London visit to be a blind alley. But he plunged into it nevertheless.

'Doing my thing. When I wasn't at the museum sketching a group of Harriers – Montague's and Pallid, if you want the details – I was being bored to the eyeballs with the weather.'

'You found yourself some female company? Forgive me, I remember a similar occasion...'

'You would. You coppers thrive on muckraking. You file it away and bring it up to confound the innocent.'

'Hardly the innocent,' Rogers said cheerfully, 'but otherwise yes. It all goes into a computer these days. And we don't make the muck. It rubs off from people like you.' He rasped the bristles pushing through the skin of his jowls with the back of his hand. 'If you didn't get yourself a woman, what were you doing about being bored?'

'I drank. I can give you the name of the bar if you want it.'

'I'll ask you later if I think it important.' He smiled again. 'I understand you did some bird painting at the Nortons' place.'

There was a quite marked searching for words. 'Yes. The Bonelli's Eagle and a Cooper's Hawk. An accommodating couple, the Nortons.'

'Particularly Mrs Norton,' Rogers said without expression.

Quint narrowed his good eye. 'Just what does that mean?'

Rogers was bland. 'Norton – as I believe you know

perfectly well – was also a client of Nancy's. Mrs Norton knows this. *Ipso facto*, being still his wife, she must be accommodating.' Rogers eyed him closely. 'You look peaked,' he said. 'Can I get you something?'

Quint leaned back on the chaise-longue, brushing invisible cobwebs from his face. It looked scrubbed of its tan. His cigar stub lay unheeded and cold, having burned a scar on the table at his side. 'Brandy . . . in the sideboard. I took a fair beating from that mad assistant of yours.'

Rogers, rising, reacted sharply. 'I told you once before. He'd resigned. He's no assistant of mine.' He slid back the doors of the sideboard and found a bottle of four-star cognac. He poured an alcoholic's idea of a stiff drink into a balloon glass and handed it to Quint, holding it carefully by the stem.

'Take one for yourself,' Quint said.

Rogers didn't bother to answer. When Quint had drained the glass he took it from him by the stem, putting it unobtrusively out of Quint's reach.

'Better?' he asked, reseating himself.

Quint nodded.

'Tell me about Lingard.'

A spasm of distaste crossed the lean face. 'All right. I returned by the last train tonight, picking up my car and getting back about . . .' he looked at his wrist watch '. . . three-quarters of an hour ago. I hadn't been here five minutes when Lingard opened the door and just walked in.' Quint's features assumed the expression he had used against the intruder. It wasn't a welcoming one. 'I asked him what the hell he wanted.'

'You recognized him, of course.'

'I recognized him all right. I demanded to see his warrant. That's when he said he wasn't here as a police officer. He said "I am justice." It sounded silly and I thought he was being funny.'

171

'I don't think he was. He'd started up in business on his own account in the administration of justice.'

Quint made a noise in his throat. 'Whatever his reason, he asked me what I'd done to Nancy. His eyes were odd, staring, you know, not focused. I said, "What the devil! Get out! I haven't done anything to the bloody woman." He yelled at me then. "You raped her, you filthy bastard! Then dumped her like a sack of offal!" He came closer to me and before I caught on had hit me in the face with the flat of his hand. It knocked me backwards, ass over tit. I looked at him from down on the floor. He had *tears* in his eyes.' Quint shuddered. 'That frightened me more than anything else. I knew he was round the twist and – like I told you – as crazy as an elephant in *must*. It's a horrible thing to be up against somebody who's insane. I tried to wriggle away but he jammed his foot on my trouser leg, pinning me down.' He stirred on the plush of the chaise-longue. 'Give me another cigar, will you?' When he was drawing deeply at it, he continued, 'I didn't need to have much of an IQ to know the man was an expert at whatever he was doing. He grabbed me and pulled me upright with one hand, hitting me again with the other. As easily as if I'd been a baby. He shouted, "You were with her on Sunday! She was in your car!"' Quint's mouth turned down at the corners. 'On the same theme as you are now. I told him not to be so bloody stupid.' His nostrils rotated in the anguish of his recollection. 'So he hit me again. Somehow I managed to knee him in the gut and run for the telephone. I never made it. Not by yards. I felt this dreadful pain in the side of my neck and I tumbled over a chair on to the floor, twisting my arm and feeling something crack. I was paralysed down one side. He kept shouting, "You raped her, you bastard, you must have done. Tell me you did or I'll kill you." He pulled me upright again and did this.' Quint touched his swollen eye. 'I was getting to the point where I was going to say I had and chance what he did. That was when I heard a banging – I believe at the door – and must have flaked out. I can't even remember whether he hit me again. Then one of your chaps was lifting me on to this settee . . .' His mouth was ugly. 'I want him charged.'

'He will be. Whether you want it or not. Who told you about Nancy's death?'

'Lingard.'

Rogers shook his head. 'You're not curious enough about the details. Somebody else filled you in.'

'It was in the newspapers.'

'Not in the national press, it wasn't. And not in the local papers until after you'd left. You,' he said positively, 'have been in touch with someone knowing a lot about it, haven't you?'

'Believe me, chief inspector, you're on the wrong track.'

'All right. So put me on the right one.'

'I can't if I don't know.'

'That's a pity,' Rogers said, 'because I'm going to arrest you on suspicion of having committed an arrestable offence.'

Quint flinched and his head jerked. 'An arrestable offence?' he echoed feebly.

'Breaking and entering Nancy Frail's flat will do for a start. I can think of another,' he added grimly.

'Jesus wept! You *can't*.'

'Famous last words, Quint. I can and I am. There's a finger impression on the door-post that might just put you there.' He did not miss the shadow of unease crossing Quint's face.

'It could have been there since God knows when.'

'That isn't the opinion of the chap finding it. He says it's fresh. I assume you're not going to object to our taking your fingerprints for a comparison?'

Quint raised a small flicker of protest. 'I am indeed going to object.'

'All right. I can always get a magistrate's order to take them by force,' Rogers pointed out equably. 'It takes time, that's all. Your time.' He glanced at the brandy glass. 'But don't worry. I'll probably find all I want on that.'

'That's a dirty underhanded trick.'

'I know a thousand of them,' Rogers said unruffled. 'I use them against the dirty underhanded people I have to deal with.'

The telephone bell rang. Rogers went to it before Quint could object and lifted the receiver to his ear. 'Yes,' he said. There was a moment of light-breathing silence and then the purring sound of a disconnection. 'Guess who,' he said sardonically to Quint.

Quint stretched out his good arm. 'Let me make a call.'

'Of course.' Rogers trailed the handset to him.

Quint placed it on the chaise-longue beside him, carefully turning the dialling face away from the detective. Then, with the receiver pressed hard against his ear, he dialled a five-figure number, using the thumb of his injured arm and keeping his eyes on Rogers, grimacing the discomfort of it. After listening for a few moments, he asked, 'Did you call?' Receiving an answer, he said, 'I am being interviewed by Chief Inspector Rogers so do not call me again. I have said nothing. Neither have I mentioned your name. So do not allow yourself to be told I have.' He replaced the receiver quickly and stared defiantly at Rogers.

If he expected an angry reaction from the detective he was disappointed. Rogers' expression was amused. 'Not particularly clever,' he said. 'And you'll never know how helpful you've been. Had you a key to the flat?'

Quint snorted. 'You flatter me.'

'Is that why you had to break open the door?'

'It's your theory. It isn't a very good one.'

'We'll soon know. This other woman who isn't Nancy Frail and who telephones you with all the latest news. Who is she?'

Quint tightened his lips.

Rogers was deadly serious. 'It might be in your own best interests to tell me.'

'No.' Quint had chewed the end of the cigar soggy and brown nicotine tar stained his teeth. He pulled a face and rubbed his handkerchief over them.

'You're protecting her,' Rogers said. 'Because she's a married woman?' He watched closely Quint's expression. 'Ah! Because she's one of your ...'

'Shut up! Don't say it,' Quint interrupted forcefully. 'Don't even think it.'

Rogers was unimpressed. 'I *am* thinking it,' he said flatly. 'What in the hell else would I think? If I'm anything, I'm surprised.'

Quint was bitter. 'Like I said before, you policemen never forget, do you? Never put anything but the worst construction on things.'

'We're logical. The background's the man so far as we're concerned. And it fits. All I'm getting from you are evasions. Innocent men don't evade issues. Tell me about this woman,' he persisted. 'Is she the one you chucked Nancy for?'

Quint was weary. 'Where's that bloody doctor? I could be dying for all he cares.'

'He's on the way,' Rogers assured him. 'I don't suppose he stands in his drive in running shorts and spiked shoes just on the offchance he gets a message you've broken a fetlock. It's foggy and the poor bugger might have been in bed.'

'Funny man,' Quint said sourly.

'You know Park Dominis, of course?'

'In detail. Nancy talked about the conniving bastard *ad nauseam.*'

'He's dead.' Rogers watched his eyes.

Quint's head jerked and more ash dropped on his tie. 'Dead!' he repeated feebly, bewilderment on his face. His jaw muscles knotted in small bunches.

'I should have said murdered,' Rogers corrected himself. 'Although, at a pinch and with a smart alec barrister, it could be bulldozed into manslaughter.'

'Oh, Christ!' His one open pale eye hunted the room as if seeking the answer on the walls. He was paper-white and seemed shrunken, his suit made for a bigger man.

'Your Intelligence Section didn't tell you that? Not even that he was missing?'

Quint merely looked stunned.

'Didn't you see him outside the flat on Sunday evening? He was there.'

Quint groaned. 'What a mess . . .'

'Yes.' Rogers applied a match to his dead pipe and puffed smoke. 'Let's see if we can guess at what happened. I want you to know, to appreciate, exactly what you've let yourself in for. Go back to Sunday evening. Nancy and the man we'll call X were having their usual little romp in bed. It wasn't her own bed, of course. Had it been, none of X's troubles would have happened. She, at least, was starkers. When you pay for it, I suppose you can insist on the full treatment *au naturel*. In all this scrabbling around, Nancy suffered a fatal thrombosis, leaving X in an excruciatingly embarrassing position. A naked dead woman in one's bed takes some explaining away and X didn't propose to do any explaining. He's that sort of a man. After unsuccessfully trying to revive her with brandy, he dressed her as best he could in the clothing she had taken off. And that's a quite different proposition from undressing a live, co-operative woman. It shows.'

176

Quint, leaning forward, had covered his forehead with his hand, concealing his eyes. His cigar, wedged between his fingers, had gone out.

Rogers continued, 'I assume now that X, with a fair amount of reckless desperation, carried poor dead Nancy outside and into the passenger seat of the car in which she arrived. Which means,' he said pointedly, 'the man was on his own in the house. He could hardly do what he did with a woman wandering about on the premises. And that's an important point. What X didn't know was that Dominis was prowling around playing detective, trying to catch him and Nancy at it. Whether he saw X carrying the body or driving her in the car remains for X to say. I'm going to assume the latter because there's little doubt that X – in a moment of horrible panic at being caught red-handed or later, from sheer bloody-minded vicious-ness – ran the car at Dominis and did him in. So X found himself with two bodies to dispose of. Each connected to the other by an obvious association, hating each other in life, brought together in death. You're with me so far, Quint?' he asked politely.

Quint uncovered his eyes for a brief moment. They looked sick. 'You're a sadistic bastard,' he mumbled.

'Just an informative one,' Rogers said. 'Where was I? Yes, with two bodies. We'll assume X hid Dominis tem-porarily and got on with his plan to dispose of Nancy. The lane isn't too far away from his home. It hasn't to be because it is necessary for him to walk back. Once there, he put Nancy in the driver's seat of her car, hoping that the police with their well-known ability at jumping to conclusions might assume she had driven to the lane and died at the wheel. What we were supposed to make of the holes in the windscreen, God only knows. Woodworm or termite infestation, possibly. But X is a reasonably cool customer. He wasn't going to cart a blood-soaked Dominis around in his own car and provide the police with lots of scientific evidence to use against him. He looked for and found Dominis's car, put his body into it and drove to the moor. He probably thought it a good idea to dump the whole caboodle down a hole until he realized he had to get back to town. So it was Dominis only who was put down and his car driven back and abandoned. Again, within reasonable walking distance of X's home.' Rogers' expression was unsmiling. 'A nasty little story, eh? And somewhere you fit into it. So why shouldn't I assume X has a need to visit Nancy's flat. Perhaps to recover some incriminating papers.' He cocked his head. 'Or something else?'

Quint shook his head blindly. 'No,' he whispered.

Rogers shrugged. He had all the indifference of a man knowing his own mind. 'It's a tenable theory. And it'll do until I get something different. The irony of it all is that Dominis wasn't her legal husband. The records at Somerset House say she was still married to an American called Swerdloff...'

There was the sound of a car on the gravel outside, crawling along in bottom gear. Rogers went to the window and peered through the curtains. 'Here comes your doctor,' he said coldly. 'You'd better do some serious thinking between now and when he discharges you into our custody.'

Although he received no reply, Rogers was content. He knew precisely where he was going and what he had to do.

15

Seated at his desk, Rogers stared at the telephone handset in front of him for a long time. Without removing the receiver he dialled the number 23222, listening carefully to the clicking of the spring return mechanism, reproducing the delays he had heard in Quint's own dialling of his call.

Satisfied, he uncradled the receiver and dialled the number again. When a woman's voice answered, he said, 'Rogers here, Miss Wallace. Are you on your own?'

There was an indrawing of breath at the other end. 'Yes.'

'I thought you would want me to let you know Mr Quint has been interviewed concerning the death of Miss Frail.'

'I ... I'm surprised ...'

'I'm sure you aren't, Miss Wallace,' he said matter-of-factly. 'He telephoned you less than thirty minutes ago.' When she made no objection to that, he added, 'He's in custody.'

'Oh .' It was a punctured sound. 'Can ... can I ask on what charge?'

'There are two. The first is in connection with the breaking into her flat.' He heard the sound again. 'The second is a much more serious charge.'

'I don't understand ...'

'It relates to my enquiries into the murder of Park Dominis. Miss Frail's husband.'

She made the sort of noise that comes from trembling lips. Then she whispered, 'Please say it isn't true, Mr Rogers.'

'He's dead, Miss Wallace.' He was gentle with her now.

'Killed by the same man who drove Miss Frail to the lane and left her there. And you know who that was.'

'Oh, God!' she moaned. 'What are you *saying*?' He imagined her holding herself from collapsing only by her courage and a need to know.

'It's true.'

There was a long, unhappy silence. Finally she said, 'Mr Rogers, I honestly didn't know. He didn't tell me ...'

'It should make a difference, shouldn't it? About protecting him, I mean.'

'Yes.' Her whisper was muffled by the grey dust of defeat. 'How was he killed?'

'He was run down by Miss Frail's car. Then thrown into a hole on the moors.'

'It ... it could have been accidental?'

'If it was, the distinction didn't help Dominis very much.'

'He wouldn't do it.' Her protest wasn't strong enough.

'Yes, he would. He did.'

There was a long silence. 'You wouldn't lie to me, Mr Rogers? Harry said ...'

He interrupted her, a cutting edge to his stern voice. 'I know exactly what he said. I was there. What I'm telling you is that I've spent an hour or so pulling Dominis out of a pothole. I'm unlikely to be anything but very serious about it.'

'Forgive me, Mr Rogers,' she said quietly. 'I accept that.'

'And I accept you won't want to stick to the fiction of your being in on Sunday evening. Not knowing what I've now told you.'

'What can I say?' She was spiritless, beaten; her words dead flowers on a grave.

'The truth might be a good idea.'

'I thought ... only her. She was dead ... the scandal ... it didn't seem that serious ...'

'I knew you'd lied to me. But not why.'

'I didn't lie, Mr Rogers. Not directly.'

'Perhaps not,' he said ironically, 'but very much the next best thing. You were ambiguous.'

'I'm sorry . . .'

'You'll tell me now?'

'I have no choice.'

'No, you haven't.'

Her forlornness came through clearly. 'Oh, God. Andrew . . .'

'I'll come straight away.'

'Please . . . no. I'll come to you. I can't stay here.'

'Where is your brother?'

'He's attending a Farmers' Union dinner.'

'I'll be waiting.' He dropped the receiver on its cradle thoughtfully.

He spoke to the Chief Constable at his home. Huggett sounded like a man who wanted nothing more than to stay in bed and put his head under the pillow in the hope that the nastiness would all be gone by the morning.

While he waited for Constance Wallace, Rogers co-ordinated the eating of cardboard-thin cheese sandwiches from the canteen with a quick wash and a brushing of his stained clothing. He also found the time to mow his darkening chin and jowls and stick pink tape over his grazed knuckles. When he moved, pain twinged in the shoulder joint where Lingard had kicked him. There wasn't much he could do about the depression of his spirits.

He visited the chargeroom to sign the sheet authorizing Lingard's detention, glancing at his late colleague with a face of stone but feeling, beneath it, a deep pity for his hunched and silent wretchedness.

Quint, being splinted and bandaged in the Casualty Department of the hospital, was not injured seriously enough to be hospitalized – as he had no doubt hoped – and would shortly be joining Lingard in the cells.

A quick brushing of Quint's brandy glass with mercuric-oxide powder had produced the twin of the finger impression found on the door-post of Nancy Frail's flat.

When Constance Wallace arrived, the perfume of gin hung around her like a cloud of invisible smoke. She was sheep-skinned and tweeded; accoutred as if she had freshly come from the hunting and killing of an otter. The fog had left diamond points of moisture in her hair. Her expression was fixed and unsmiling; her eyes raw-rimmed from crying. Her voice had lost the pink wholesomeness it possessed on their first meeting. Rogers had noticed suitcases on the back seat of the car in which she arrived.

Before she accepted his invitation to sit in the chair at the side of his desk, she handed him an envelope.

He opened it and took out a blob of cottonwool. In it was a tiny curved lens. It looked as fragile as paper ash. He held it shining and dry in the hollow of his palm. 'Where, Miss Wallace?'

'Mrs Jacobs found it on the stair carpet and handed it to me.' She was seated with her legs tight together, her hands folded in an attitude of apparent submission.

'You knew it to be Miss Frail's?'

'Not at first. But I guessed, of course.' She was brooding on her fingernails, not meeting his regard.

'You told your brother?'

'No. There was no point. Not after he asked me to tell you I had been at home all evening.'

'It also suited your own purpose.' Rogers' cheeks were hard-planed and purposeful.

'Yes. But I don't think I would have gone that far for myself.'

He remained silent until she was forced to look at him.

'You were in the car when Quint stole the Rajput painting from Miss Frail's flat,' he said.

'What Harry did, he did for me,' she protested, as if that whitewashed the act. For her it obviously did. She was, Rogers concluded, in love with the man.

He showed his teeth. 'The law doesn't recognize that sort of altruism.'

'We didn't regard it as stealing, Mr Rogers. My brother had no right to give it away.'

'Legally he did.'

'But not morally.'

'No,' he agreed, wagging his head. 'Probably not. Anyway, a claim of right made in good faith is always a good defence. You knew she would be with your brother that evening?'

She gave an exhalation of contempt. 'Yes. He always made it clear when I should be out. I suppose because I didn't like her and made no secret of it.'

'This happened monthly?'

'Yes. You knew?'

'She kept a record of their meetings. There was a visit due for October.'

'I see. So that's how you knew about Andrew?'

'Partly. Do you like your brother?' His chin pressed on the knot of his tie.

'That's an odd question . . . not a very nice one.' Hauteur was not far away.

'Do you?'

She considered a second or two and submissiveness came back. 'Not enough to lie for him any more. Not if Harry has to suffer.'

'I didn't think you would. Did he know about you and Quint?'

'No.'

'And if he had?'

'He would have objected.' Her lip curled. It was a soft, pink, attractive lip. 'It might have interfered with my housekeeping for him.'

Rogers understood, although in his experience it was usually a selfish mother who kept her daughter chained to her needs. 'Wasn't he curious where you went?'

She laughed mirthlessly. 'Not in the slightest. Just so long as I came back.' She snapped open her handbag and withdrew a flat green leather case. 'May I smoke?'

He stood and reached across, holding the flame of his lighter to the cigarette between her lips. That near he could feel the heat of her body and smell both the odour of her femininity and the gin with which she had fortified herself against him.

Seated again, he filled and lit his pipe, tasting gratefully the narcotic woodiness of the smoke. 'You knew of Miss Frail's actual relationship with your brother?'

'I suspected, naturally. But it wasn't anything he was likely to discuss with me.' She licked her lips shiny as if needing more gin. 'And I wasn't interested enough to care. I knew he would never marry her.'

'Tell me, Miss Wallace, what happened Sunday evening.'

She looked at her fingernails again. 'We knew Andrew was expecting her because he'd asked me was I going to be out. So we waited outside until she arrived and . . . and was obviously going to remain. Then we went to Queen Anne's Road and waited again, making sure there was nobody about. Then Harry stopped the car just short of her flat and I waited in it. He was gone for only a few minutes and returned with my Rajput. We both felt dreadfully guilty about what we'd done. Then we went to Harry's house. When I returned home at midnight, Miss Frail had left and my brother was in his room.'

'What if you had returned earlier?'

'I never did.' Her big breasts pushed against the stuff of her tweed dress. 'It was expected I would remain out until then.'

'And assuming Miss Frail had returned to her flat and discovered the painting missing?'

'My brother had never told me he'd given it to her. He could hardly tax me with its taking.'

'How did you know she had it?'

She shrugged. 'He wouldn't have given it to anyone else.'

'And where is it now?'

'In my bedroom.'

'When did you first suspect all was not well?'

'Not until Andrew spoke to me. After your visit.'

'Not when Mrs Jacobs gave you the contact lens?'

She made a moue, her brown eyes scornful. 'That meant only what I already knew.'

'You looked concerned when I first called.'

'I was. I thought you'd called about the painting.'

'After I'd spoken to your brother, what happened?'

'He told me Miss Frail had died of a heart attack while they were talking. That in order to avoid a misunder-standing, a terrible scandal, he had taken her in her car to a quiet lane and left her there. He assured me he had done nothing criminal. That his position as a magistrate, even his knighthood, would be in jeopardy. That she was dead and nothing could alter that.' Her mouth twisted. 'He pleaded the good name of grandfather . . . our own posi-tion in the community.' There was a self-deprecation in the down-turning of her mouth. Rogers could visualize the whining cowardice of the man. 'And, as you have pointed out, my own motives weren't entirely selfless. If taking the painting was serious enough before, it became infinitely more so when I knew she was dead. Not wholly for myself. Harry would have been in a worse position. As he now appears to be. You yourself confirmed she had died naturally so I allowed you to believe I had been at home all evening.' She looked lost. 'I didn't think for one moment that anything else was involved – certainly not the death of Mr Dominis – or that Harry would be suspected.'

'Isn't that why he went to London?'

She was surprised. 'No. He'd arranged that long before. He left before either of us knew anything of her death.'

'But you told him later? By telephone.'

'Yes. I couldn't contact him until late this afternoon. When I did he returned by the first available train. He isn't the sort of man to avoid trouble at the expense of another.'

'No, he probably isn't,' Rogers agreed. 'And to his credit he hasn't involved you in any way. But he knows now what you and he have let yourselves in for and is busy thinking of an out for you both. He'll have put two and two together and come up with the name Sir Andrew Wallace.'

She sucked smoke into her lungs. 'It's a terrible thing to contemplate, Mr Rogers. That one's brother murd . . . killed someone.'

'People who do these things are always another's brother; another's father, mother or sister.' *Which*, thought Rogers in retrospect, *wasn't very consoling.*

'Dominis was watching Miss Frail,' he said. 'Trying to get evidence for a divorce.' He saw her wince. 'You didn't see him when you were waiting outside your own place?'

She shook her head. 'No. Please tell me. Did Andrew . . . was what he did deliberate?'

'I don't honestly know. Who knows what's in a man's mind?'

'Why did you think Harry had killed him?'

'I never said I did. I said his detention related to it. It is,

186

in fact, a charge of impeding the arrest or prosecution of your brother. Not,' he admitted, 'a charge now likely to be pursued but one you may face yourself.'

That wasn't worrying her and she stared at him with her grandfather's empire-building eyes. 'You *knew* Harry didn't kill him.'

'I was fairly certain he hadn't.'

'You trapped me, misled me, in a way.' She screwed her cigarette to extinction in an ashtray.

'You misled yourself, Miss Wallace,' he said with coldness in his words. 'It would be ludicrous to suggest anyone could improperly trap a person into telling the truth. Blame your brother if you must blame someone. He used you and, in using you, must have realized you would become involved in more than the concealment of Miss Frail's death.'

'Whatever I feel about him,' she said dully, 'he's my brother . . .'

He spoke gently. 'I shan't use as evidence what you have told me. Nor need he know you have spoken to me. Mrs Jacobs' evidence of her finding of the contact lens will be enough to put Miss Frail in the house. The rest follows inevitably.'

'I've already told him.' She was looking at a point a million light-years outside the walls of his office.

Rogers was startled and raised his black eyebrows. 'You have?'

'I left a note on his desk. I can't go back now.'

He frowned. 'What did you say?'

'Just that I was coming to you. That I was telling the truth.'

'When is he due back?'

She lifted the cuff of the sheepskin coat and looked at her watch. It was a tiny thing on a gold strap. 'He should be there now.'

187

Rogers pulled the telephone handset to him and dialled 23222. He waited, listening to the call signal repeating itself unheard in an empty room. Then he replaced it. 'Not yet,' he told her.

'It won't make any difference,' she said. 'I'd still tell him. I'd have told him personally had he been there. I'm going away with Harry.'

'But not yet.'

'What do you mean?'

'You'll stay here until I've seen your brother.' He said it with the calm assurance of unarguable authority. 'If, after that, things are as you say, I'll release Quint on bail. I don't think either of you need worry too much about the charges.'

'No?' She was subdued and introspective. 'But that's not all of it. Isn't there a name for a female counterpart of Judas Iscariot, Mr Rogers?'

'That's ridiculous,' he said harshly. 'And maudlin. You flatter your brother. I don't see anything Christ-like in dumping a dead girl – if she *was* dead – and running down her poor devil of a husband when he's caught doing it. And I don't think the grand-daughter of General Napier Wallace does either.'

That kind of gooey morality against informing on criminals always irritated Rogers to blasphemy.

16

'How did we do it?' Coltart asked, sitting at Rogers' side. In his stolid way he was being heavily sarcastic. They were in Rogers' car, driving cautiously through the thickening fog to Spye Green Hall. 'You played this one pretty close to your chest.'

'That's because I was doing a lot of guessing. If I was proved wrong I wanted to be wrong on my own.'

Coltart's eyes glittered his humour. 'And to be able to say how good you are when you turned out to be right.'

'Do I look that smug?'

'Yes.'

Rogers laughed. 'I don't mean to. It's probably a nervous tic. But I had nothing really. Only some scientific bric-à-brac that added up to very little. Not things that put a label on the man who did it but rather one that eliminated the others. And,' he added sourly, 'I'd had a gutful of gossip and defensive ambiguities from nearly everybody I interviewed. Even in a dirty country like we're living in now, men still don't like to admit they pay for it.'

Coltart chewed his toothpick, nodding his head in agreement at Rogers' opinion of the intransigence of witnesses.

'First of all, we knew it was a big man who drove Frail to the lane.' The windscreen wipers were sweeping triangles of transparency on the glass and Rogers occasionally pushed his head forward, sometimes tapping the bowl of his pipe against it.

'We did?' The car was filling with smoke and Coltart kept his face as near the crack of open window as he could without giving offence.

'The driver's seat was ratcheted back to its limit. I tried it for size and it suited me. *She* wouldn't have been able to drive it like that. Her feet wouldn't reach the pedals. Then there was Dominis's car. He's a big man and the seat was already adjusted to suit him. A smaller man driving it would have needed to pull it forward. So, in a negative way, I could eliminate Norton and Galbraith. Both men with their bottoms nearer the ground than average.'

'Leaving Wallace, Quint and Hacker.'

'And Lingard. I never forgot him.' Rogers braked sharply and swerved, nearly colliding with the rear of an unlit parked van.

'Bastard!' he swore absentmindedly. Glowing flakes of tobacco dropped unheeded on to his lap. 'He was in love with the woman and, I'll bet, the only one who hadn't done his thing with her. Even had he, he's a bachelor and there'd have been no overwhelming reason for him to dump her if she'd died on him. No,' he said reflectively, 'although I never overlooked the possibility, it was his flailing around like the Arm of the Lord that worried me. Hacker didn't fit in, either. If she'd had a coronary in his bed he'd have most likely written to *The News of the World* about it. And he was much too forthcoming about a similar instance of Dominis keeping tag on him. That would have been a far too sensitive point to bring up had he been involved. Whatever else he said, he'd have skated past that. And a town flat. I just couldn't see him carting bodies about in the Regent Crescent. Even on a Sunday evening. Asking his girl-friend to confirm he was at the Acey-Deucey Club was very much a formality.'

'Quint?' Coltart prompted.

'H'm. Quint could have cleared himself in five minutes. At the expense of Constance Wallace. Which gives him a decency I never suspected. He hadn't seen Frail for over four months. So why suddenly last Sunday? I would have accepted he'd got her out of his system by then. What is certain is that he'd called at her flat. And, as we now know, left his dab on the door-post. The by-product of all this is that the man who very carefully wiped Frail's car clean of prints isn't likely to leave one on a door he'd just forced open. As a corollary, Quint's breaking into the flat meant that the woman with him couldn't have been Frail. Wallace had given her a Rajput painting and it was missing. To me that signified Constance Wallace. And if it was

Constance Wallace, then she had lied about being at home.' He yawned with his teeth clenched on the pipe stem. 'And lying about it meant her brother had something to hide. Of course, she could have lied to avoid being suspected of stealing the Rajput. But it left her brother very much on his own, having produced a lie for an alibi at the second time of asking. He panicked badly there. Unnecessarily too. You don't have to produce an alibi just because you're asked. All I had to do was to allow his sister to believe Quint was in serious trouble, to let her know there was more to it than just the dumping of a dead girl. She had a choice then and being the woman she is, she made the proper one. The one she thought her grandfather would have made.'

He changed gear to take the gradient of Rooks Hill. It was one o'clock and the streets were dead and cold. Even the cats seemed to be staying indoors.

'Quint thought he was being clever in telephoning her, warning her to keep quiet. But dialling a number with three twos on the end of it was almost as obvious as if I'd been looking over his shoulder. It was too much of a coincidence. He had to be speaking to her.'

'What evidence have we against Wallace?'

Rogers frowned. 'Nothing much. I'm not likely to get the Detective of the Year Award over it. I'm guessing that Dominis was killed in the drive of Spye Green Hall. If so, we should find something there. He probably saw Wallace carrying Frail's body out. He'd be baffled, not knowing what was happening. She could have been drunk for all he knew. But Dominis was, by all accounts, a man short on temper and long on action. It's not difficult to imagine him wondering what the hell and then, when he saw Wallace bundle her in the car and start to drive it, to charge out to try and stop his evidence for a divorce getting away from him. I can see Wallace panicking – I can't believe he'd do it coldbloodedly – and driving the car at him, crushing him against the gate pillar. Dominis's upper half would shoot forward over the bonnet, his head going smack through the windscreen, leaving one of his hairs on Frail's lap. To use the car, Wallace would have to punch himself another hole in the driver's side. I noticed the gravel had been freshly raked at the entrance and I've no doubt we'll find bits of glass there.' Rogers shook his head. 'But dear God! What bad luck he had. First she died in his house. Naked and probably in his bed. That would be enough to stun most men. On top of that Dominis had to be watching outside and is killed in the ensuing panic. Talk about troubles compounding themselves into disaster. Anyway, apart from the contact lens that's about the lot.' He pulled a face in the darkness. 'And you know how far that'd take us against the sort of barrister Wallace can afford. All he'd need to say is that she left him – after a cosy little chat about French stamps – alive and happy : that she died elsewhere under circumstances which only God and somebody else knows about.'

'It doesn't sound very convincing,' Coltart said dubiously.

Rogers looked sideways with a crooked smile. 'Since when did any defence have to? It needs only throw doubt on the facts and some mud at the prosecution's witnesses and acquittal's a certainty.'

'What about the contact lens?'

'On a stair carpet? So she went upstairs to use the toilet, to wash her hands. Any reason but that of going to bed will do.'

'And she drives her car away one-eyed?'

'If she lost a lens, she lost it. It needn't immobilize her.'

'So what are you going to do?'

'Question him. And tell him at the same time he needn't answer unless it pleases him to do so.' He snorted disgust.

'And if he decides to remain mute?'

'I shall probably get stuffy and point out that innocence claims the right of speaking, as guilt invokes the privilege of silence. Jeremy Bentham said that first,' he added, 'not me.'

'That'll shake him,' Coltart said ironically.

'He'll go white with fear,' Rogers said with equal irony. 'Anyway, it won't be the first murder case undetected because the murderer won't confide in us.' He made it sound as if frustration and failure were an acceptable part of the job. But for him they weren't. There was a deep need in him to ensure that justice was done. Anything else made what he did pointless.

With Coltart holding his torch and shielding its light with a flap of his overcoat, Rogers stooped over the gravel and sifted it through his fingers with the care of a miner prospecting for diamonds. He felt no more than a deserved satisfaction when he found the few tiny cubes of glass with which the laboratory would place Nancy Frail's car and the smashing of its windscreen firmly in Wallace's driveway.

Pulling aside a freshly planted cotoneaster bush, he exposed a fresh unweathered scar, made at the height of a car's bumper, in the sandstone of the gate pillar.

'We seem to be on the winning side, sergeant,' Rogers whispered, wiping dampness from his hands with his handkerchief. 'Let's take our fortunes on the flood.'

The house was silent except for a low, hardly perceptible murmur that sounded as if it were purring like a gigantic squatting cat. A thin light shone from between the edges of the curtains of Wallace's study, diffusing itself into the fog as soft yellow motes of luminescence.

Rogers rapped the big door knocker and waited, shoulder to shoulder with Coltart. The insistent mutter of sound was louder now and all around them, the blanket-ing fog muffling the location of its source although they felt the tremors of it pulsing up through the soles of their shoes.

When the house remained silent, unanswering, Rogers untwisted the handle and opened the door, the two men stepping inside. The warm parched breath of central heat-ing hit them as they closed the door. The hall was illumin-ated by the light from the study reflecting through its open door. Apart from the low murmur that had followed them inside the house, there was the absolute unbreathing quietness of an unoccupied building.

The study was empty. A screwed-up ball of grey lay on the carpet. Rogers went in and retrieved it, unfolding the stiff parchment paper. He read aloud the message written on it for Coltart's information:

'Andrew: I'm sorry. I cannot go on with it. I am going to see Mr Rogers and tell him the truth. I shall not be coming back. Constance.'

Rogers stepped to the door of the study and called into the emptiness of the house. 'Sir Andrew! Sir Andrew!'

He waited, listening; a dark premonition creeping up on him. Then recognition of the vibration and under-standing came into his eyes. He cried sharply, 'The garage!', plunging along the hall and out into the fog, his shoes skidding as he raced along the wet cement walk to the rear of the house. Coltart was close behind, panting down the back of his neck.

The garage door was closed, the silver disc of a yale key glinting from its lock. From behind the aluminium panels came the throbbing they had heard before. Rogers grasped the handle, jerked it and swung the door up and over. The garage contained a blue fog of its own. Wallace's Daimler stood in it with the interior courtesy lights shining; its engine trembling the metallic lustre of its silver flanks and shivering the loose flesh of its owner's dead jowls.

He lay limp in the driver's seat with the window down, one hand hooked by its wrist on the steering wheel. The silk lapels of his dinner jacket and the rumpled white shirt front were stained with the brown liquid still dribbling from his open mouth. He was peering forward as if checking the petrol gauge and worrying that there wouldn't be enough. On the inside of the windscreen, still ghostly visible in the drying condensation, he had written with the pad of his finger, *An accident . . .*

Holding his breath against the harshness of the exhaust fumes, his eyes stinging with acid tears, Rogers leaned into the car and cut the engine. He coughed and spat on the oil-stained floor. Wallace's skin was cherry pink and the detective, having seen too many dead men, knew any first-aid to be a waste of time. Nor had he ever considered mouth-to-mouth resuscitation a viable proposition with anyone not female and under fifty.

'He's chickened out,' Coltart rumbled disparagingly over his shoulder. He despised suicides.

Rogers walked out into the open air. The fog tasted clean and uncomplicated. He fumbled in his coat pockets for his pipe and oiled-silk pouch. 'He panicked for the third and last time,' he said, a sliver of compassion in his voice. He stuffed tobacco in the pipe bowl, not looking to do it. It was something he could do in his sleep and, were the paraphernalia of his addiction normally handy to his bed, probably would. 'I think his image was a front that held the rest of him together. Take it away and he was morally short-arsed with pomposity instead of guts.' Thinking he might be overly uncharitable to a dead man, he added, 'Of course, he might have liked Frail more than we imagined.' He didn't sound as if he believed it himself.

He nodded in the direction of Wallace. 'Does this sort of ending depress you?'

'No,' the uncomplicated Coltart said, not really understanding why it should. 'It's cowardly but it tidies things up. Saves a lot of argument.'

Rogers sighed. Soon Nancy Frail, stored waiting in the bank of refrigerated green-enamelled drawers in the anteroom to the mortuary, would be joined by Dominis and Wallace. Rogers thought that if there was anything in the theory of survival after death, they could fight out their differences somewhere other than where he would be required to worry about them.

His own worries were earthy and more pressing. His biggest problem was, he knew, that he lived too much with those posed by other people and too little with his own. His wife and brother-in-law hovered exasperatingly at the periphery of his concern, waiting to demand their share of his attention. Before he would find time to get round to them he knew, with the certainty of experience, that someone would have his skull cracked with a pickaxe handle or his safe rifled, his troubles becoming Rogers'.

He looked at his watch. It was one-twenty and it had been a long day. A bit too long for anything more exacting than a final word with Huggett and sleep. He was drained of any further impetus. He felt as if newly come from having had a woman: physically deflated and mentally spent with hardly steam enough left to talk. Paradoxically, he needed Bridget to refill his emptiness.

But Bridget was tomorrow. When he had sloughed off the cloying miasma of Nancy Frail's sex and the troubles she had left behind her like a deadly slime.

With Bridget it was going to be different. It always was different when you did it yourself....